Wakefield Press

Dodging the Bull

Paul Mitchell grew up in six Victorian country towns and now lives in the Melbourne suburb of Yarraville. His award winning poetry book, *Minorphysics*, was released in 2003 and his second collection, *Awake Despite the Hour*, was published in 2007. A journalist, copywriter and teacher, Paul has also worked as an attendant carer, service station console operator, wool classer and rock singer. He has two children, Hannah and Hugo, and when he's not writing he likes to read, worry, meditate, and then get on with writing again.

Also by Paul Mitchell

Poetry
Minorphysics (Interactive Publications, 2003)
Awake Despite the Hour (Five Islands Press, 2007)

Dodging the BULL

Stories by

Paul Mitchell

Wakefield
Press

For my children, Hannah and Hugo

Wakefield Press
1 The Parade West
Kent Town
South Australia 5067
www.wakefieldpress.com.au

First published 2007
Copyright © Paul Mitchell, 2007

Cover designed by Liz Nicholson, designBITE
Text designed and typeset by Clinton Ellicott, Wakefield Press
Printed and bound by Hyde Park Press, Adelaide

National Library of Australia
Cataloguing-in-publication entry

Mitchell, Paul, 1968–   .
Dodging the bull.

ISBN 978 1 86254 749 0 (pbk.).

1. Social psychology. 2. Self-perception. I. Title.

302.54

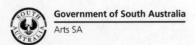
Government of South Australia
Arts SA

fox creek

Publication of this book was assisted by the
Commonwealth Government through the
Australia Council, its arts funding and advisory body.

Contents

A Grandfather's Reminder

Thanks for carrying me coffin. You were sweating on the day, there was a drip that went from your eyebrow onto your shirt. Can't have been that much trouble, I was never a heavy bugger. And there wasn't much left of me at all in the finish. I was a bag of bones.

Thanks for doing the Bible reading, too. I thought you spoke well. Can't have been easy looking out into that mob of dickheads. Everyone could smell the beer on Graeme. And Bruce. And Stewie as well. My sons. Bloody lot of pisspots. Yeah, I know you'll think that's pretty rich coming from me. But how were they? Suits smelling like mothballs and wriggling and coughing up their guts in the pews.

You did a good job. And you weren't second fiddle. Even if Steve had been alive, Nance and your mother would have chosen you because you were the only one with religion. Plus you didn't put on the waterworks. How was Stewie? I'd never have picked that. Blubbering like a girl. But tears were coming up at the back of your eyes when you joined in on 'How Great Thou Art'.

What was *that* about? For your old mate in the sky or me?

Listen, I know you were scared of me when you were a tacker. Not all the time, but sometimes. You remember that time in Rosebud? Course you do. You're never gunna forget it are ya? Never gunna let me forget it either.

I can't believe your grandmother and me ever lived in that flat. You remember it? Brown fibro and one bloody bedroom? You and your brothers slept on the floor in sleeping bags when you came for your holidays. I remember that because I used to have to whinge at you to lie down so I could still see the telly.

Shit of a joint. And Rosebud itself is the arsehole of the world, if you ask me. I think we were there because Nance wanted to keep an eye on Bruce or some bloody bullshit because he was living with a new girlfriend. She didn't think the new bird was any good for him. Probably the other way round. Anyway, it doesn't matter now.

Your mum and dad came to visit that afternoon, a few days after they'd dropped you lot off for the school holidays. You remember they were there? You bloody should, as far as I'm concerned.

You don't remember everything, ya know. Betcha don't remember that I never went to the beach. Your grandmother used to always take you, and you lot used to come back half blue and wrapped in towels, left water and sand all over the lino. But I never went to the beach after the war. Wasn't because I was always too pissed, if you're thinking it. It was because I fought on the beaches at bloody Tripoli. Couldn't ever go near a beach again after that. Didn't know that didja?

You said something smart to your mother and your dad just sat there and let you say it. I don't remember what it was. Do you? I know you remember what happened next. I dragged you outside by the ear. Then I told you to say to me what you'd said to her. I shaped up to you and told you to put your dukes up. I remember I had a smoke in my mouth and it was puffing into me eyes. You looked up at me. And I know that's all you remember. That's it, isn't it?

I didn't hit you. Just dragged you back inside and told you to apologise to your mother quick smart. You just burst into tears and she pulled you up onto her knee. The whole bloody thing only took a minute or two and about as long for me to forget it.

I was pissed. You know I was pissed. They say I was pissed every day from midday onwards. I know you've heard that. But I don't think that's quite right. Anyway, it's beside the point. I didn't hit you.

There were other times when I did though. Not in the face or anything. You'd be playing up and I'd just give you a belting to sort you out. Quite a few times, actually. When we were babysitting you lot or you were all at our place for the holidays. Can't remember that, can ya? I betcha can't. But I did. Caught my belt on your leg once and opened up a nasty little cut. Have a look at your leg. Gotta scar?

So, look, it's hard for me to say sorry for *not* hitting you. Much easier to say sorry for giving you a bloody decent whack. No one likes to belt kids these days so I could say, *Sorry, it's just how things were then.* A lot of things happened in the seventies that don't happen now. And there's no one better than D.K. Lillee these days, either. But he wasn't a patch on Keith Miller.

You can't forget it though, can you? Me standing over you with me dukes up. The thing is though, I know what your trouble is. Probably surprises you that I know. You don't think I was clued in, do you? But remember how I was the only one that knew you were gunna be a singer? You had a good voice as a young kid and I said it would only take a bit of practice and keeping off the smokes. And I was right, wasn't I?

Being clued in's not a matter of going to bloody uni, fella.

But anyway you don't need a 'sorry' from me. I could give you one though, I suppose. Here you are: sorry for dragging you out onto the lawn and scaring the shit out of you. You were only seven and when you're an adult, as you know, you forget how big you look to a kid. Mate, I had no idea you were going to remember the whole thing for the rest of your life. *Shit*, no idea at all.

I'm telling you though, I was only doing what was right, in one way. I was the head of the house – yeah, okay, the flat. It was up to me to make a move about showing you who was boss. That you couldn't talk to your mother that way. So I'm sorry that it all upset you so much, but my apology's not worth shit without one from your dad.

I might have been doing the right thing, but he had some jurisdiction didn't he? He could have stood up and said, *Hang on, I'll handle this*. I'd have let him, too. It might have been my house, but you were his kid. He could have dragged you out and given you a belt on the arse or whatever.

But he sat there and let it happen. He left ya.

I might have been pissed and cranky and a scary bastard, but I was making sure there was respect for elders in my house.

You know I love you, mate. You know it. I told you. You remember? I was lying on me bed at home, breathing through the gas mask by that stage. I told you, too, not to treat your wife and your kids like I'd treated mine. Swearing and hitting them. Throwing things at them. Wasn't easy to say that to you. Shit, you even heard me make peace with *your* mate upstairs. You saw me eyes. You know old Hughie was in there.

Listen, I've gotta go. But for Christ's sake, next time you remember yourself outside that flat, looking up at me and me fists, look up and see me eyes gone soft. Me smiling at you like I did through the mask, with me head resting back on all those pillows. Then leave me standing there, walk over to the flywire door of that shitty old flat and pull the bloody thing back. Then say, *What are ya doin, Dad? Where are ya?*

In the Shell

Five afternoons a week Jason puts on his grey pants and shirt, walks down his dirt driveway and drags his steel gate open. He walks across the road and magpies squawk on the powerlines above him while trucks groan on the distant Hume Highway.

He climbs the McPhersons' front fence and walks a couple of kilometres through two of their paddocks. He keeps an eye out for cow manure in the first and their black bull in the second. When he gets to the end of the second paddock, he climbs another fence and walks across a dirt road. Then he puffs his way up an embankment, its longer grass, until he reaches the concrete next to the yellow skip. He walks around to the front of the service station and waves through the glass at Tony, who's sitting at the console as usual, reading a newspaper. Once Tony knows he's there, Jason heads back to the skip, has a smoke and watches the sun setting like an over-ripe orange. Next to it, Mt Twyford's green is slowly turning black.

Jason throws his cigarette butt onto the concrete, grinds it senseless under his boot and walks through the Shell's automatic doors.

'How are ya, Tone?'

'Busy as batshit.'

'Look it.'

Tony folds the paper and meets Jason's eyes.

'Do anything today,' he says.

'Part from *jerk off*?' Jason offers.

'Not interested.'

'Bullshit.'

Jason thinks Tony should have at least smiled at that comment. He'd been a barrel of chuckles for the last few weeks, more than his usual jolly self – you know what they say about fat people. But he just looks down at his paper.

'Shit day?' Jason asks.

Tony looks out the window toward the highway. The top of a truck slides along the grey wall that protects some of Murchville from the noise.

'Got me mum comin to town next week.'

'Really?'

'Yeah. Her and Dad're comin down.'

Jason looks at the rack of magazines. Kylie Minogue's on one cover, looking over her shoulder at him. He looks up at Tony again, who's still staring at the highway. It's not as if his parents are strangers to the big boy, but judging by Tony's droopy face you'd think he'd been asked to put a couple of politicians up at his house for a few days.

Jason takes a magazine off the rack and flicks it. 'Buy a few beers . . . have a good one . . .'

Tony lifts his huge frame and waddles out from behind

the console. He grabs two chocolate donuts from underneath a clear plastic lid and throws some plastic coins onto
the counter.

'No worries, Tone, I'll ring it up for ya . . .'

Tony says nothing, doesn't even turn around as he heads
through the automatic doors.

'Sad sacks,' Jason whispers, watching Tony walk across
the concrete to his white Kingswood station wagon.
Behind the console, Jason slides the fake coins into his
hand and opens the register. He puts them in a special tray
for 'purchases', smiles to himself and knows they're both
good employees – the camera never lies.

He watches Tony's wagon grumble across the spillway
and onto the service road. Though he can't hear it too well
through the thick glass, he knows it will be grunting as
much as it can, heading up the entry lane's incline before
veering right onto the Hume Highway.

Jason can't see the wagon anymore, but after a kilometre
Tony will turn left and drive three kilometres before
slowing down as he comes into the Murchville sixty-zone.
Once he's pulled into his driveway, Tony will get out of the
Kingswood and drag his thirty-seven years and girth onto
his porch and through the door. He'll have a smoke in the
kitchen and leave the butt in a thin silver ashtray. Then he'll
go out to his shed and pull a red Adidas bag down from the
top of an old cupboard. He'll get back in his wagon and
drive to Mount Twyford where, by torchlight, he'll find
his normal fishing spot near the river and shoot himself
through the head with his pig-hunting rifle.

That night seven cars pull into the Shell: three late model Holdens, two Ford XR8s and one Toyota four-wheel-drive. Jason marks them all down on a piece of paper – he keeps a weekly tally and then awards a prize on Sunday to the leading car manufacturer. He keeps a tally of all the weekly prizes and awards a premiership to the winning car company at the end of the year. Last year Holden won, just, but this year Toyota's out in front of Holden with Ford not too far behind.

Jason used to give Tony the result from the day before. Now Tony takes only a passing interest in the weekly winners. After Tony's dad gave up the fruit farm, he took over a Holden dealership, before it collapsed, too, and he and his wife moved to Queensland. Half of Murchville went with them in the mid nineties, after the highway turned thick and three-laned. Then Telstra and all the banks left. Jason tells himself he'd leave, too, if there were somewhere worth going.

Tony's always talking about leaving. Jason comes into work and he's sitting there, flicking through the *Herald-Sun* job pages.

'They're lookin for console ops in Braybrook.'

Jason grabs a meat pie from the warmer and throws some fake coins on the counter.

'That'd be fucken ace, *mate*. Same crap job just busier.'

'More chicks in Melbourne.'

Jason looks at Tony's massive gut, the section rising above the console. 'Yeah,' he says, lifting an eyebrow.

'*What?* Don't you reckon I could pull the chicks in the big smoke?'

'Maybe if you can pump them up.'

It was only a rumour that Tony had a blow-up doll; Jason had never seen it.

Tony flicks through the paper.

'Be alright. Get out of this shithole.'

Jason smiles and swings his arm, motioning Tony out of the console seat and Murchville. 'Go on then. Fuck off.'

'I might,' Tony says and he picks up his blue backpack.

'You won't piss off, Tone.'

'Never know.'

It's tradition in Tony's family for the casket to be open and the body on display. But Tony's lid is closed on the altar, in the hearse and right up to the gravesite.

Jason looks around at the crowd outside the church, the people out of the woodwork for Tony's funeral. Cousins in black and dark-green suits, an aunty in white jeans smoking a long cigarette. That bloke – *Roger?* – with blond hair and tatts on his hands who used to work at the Shell. And, *Fuck*, he almost says out loud, there's even Lisa McLaren from school.

Christ, he hasn't seen her since the last day of HSC. She was dressed up as a punk that day, with a short black leather skirt and tight pink undies, not that Jason was looking. And there she is, the name-in-lights newspaper chick from Melbourne, at Tony Di Risio's funeral.

Lisa teased Tony relentlessly at high school. Now here she is with her hair dyed black – because she's *intelligent*, Jason supposes – fifth row and listening to the priest's voice echo through the church. When everyone files back onto the church steps after the service, he wants to go up and ask her what the fuck she's doing here, but he doesn't because she wouldn't remember him.

But she does – at the wake.

'Jason, how *are* you? I hear you worked with Tony ...'

'Umm ... sort of ...'

Jason sees a black leather skirt, but she's wearing dark denim jeans.

'At the Shell service station?' Lisa says, twisting her head and smiling like a teacher.

'We don't actually work together – I come in and he goes ... he *went* ... he's ...'

He looks at her.

'Gone now?' she offers, then looks at the glass of red wine in her hand.

'Yeah ...' Jason says and feels his face burning up.

She stands and looks at him as if he has a piece of chewing gum stuck under his lip. Jason doesn't ask her what or who she thinks she's looking at, but he does ask her why she's here. Stuff it, he thinks, stuck-up bitch ...

Lisa looks at him like the chewing gum is blowing a bubble by itself.

'It's the first death from our year ...'

She walks through the dark suits, jeans and dresses and sits down on a chair against the lounge-room wall. She looks across at Jason, then at the talking mob holding wine glasses and cans. She takes a pad and pen from her black bag and starts writing. She stops, looks around the room, then starts writing again.

Tony's parents waddle around with silver trays full of salami and olives, nodding their heads and accepting embraces. On the kitchen bench there's a plate of chocolate donuts, untouched. Later, Tony's mother stands in her son's quiet lounge room, next to her always-silent husband, and makes a speech about how much water Tony used to splash out of the bath when he was a little boy. She drags up a small laugh and Jason sees the cousin next to him smile. Then Tony's mum cries and everyone looks at the brown carpet or Tony's pictures of J Lo and Matthew Lloyd on the wall. A woman blows her nose and sniffs behind Jason, but everyone else is quiet, waiting to see if Tony's mum will start talking again. But she bows her head and her husband leads her away to a back bedroom. Somebody turns the stereo up again and Jason lifts his can to his mouth.

The stereo gets louder as the afternoon goes on. Lisa McLaren leaves, waving to Jason from a group of people at the door. He watches her go and tells himself that Tony had to do something pretty special to get a chick like that into his house. Wine glasses are re-filled and beer cans are scrunched into green garbage bins.

People look at each other and say, 'I can't believe it. You'd never have picked it.'

'He was always a happy bloke,' some whisper. 'He'd never hurt anyone,' the bloke with the tatts on his hands says. And Jason thinks, Well, he never did hurt anyone. Then he remembers the sealed up casket.

Jason goes to sleep that night with his head on a Melbourne Bitter spin, and dreams the Shell is a white, late-model Commodore and Tony's driving it, yelling out the window, *I've won the premiership*, and manoeuvring the station wagon onto the Hume, pointing it toward Melbourne. Then a flock of sleek Toyotas, flapping their two doors, swoop down and scrape their tyre-claws on the sides of Tony's Shell Commodore. His eyes are wide open above his big cheeks and Jason wakes up shouting. Before long he feels his eyes starting to cry, his stomach moves up and down and it's like he's listening to someone sobbing in the room next door.

Jason gets four weeks holiday a year and he'd always spend two of them in shitty Murchville hanging out with Tony.

On days that he'd normally be walking across the paddocks to the Shell, Jason would get in his Cortina, pick up a pizza he'd phone-ordered, then grab a dozen cans. He'd drive to Tony's and think, every time, *Shit*, I should have bought more pizza.

The pair would sit on brown vinyl chairs that Tony's parents gave him, along with the house to rent, when they left for Queensland. They would watch pornos until they got bored or Tony headed to the toilet – Jason would wait until he got home. Some nights they rolled a joint and Tony always let Jason take the last tug. When they smoked they always ended up in beanbags in front of music videos, eating corn chips and gabbling to each other.

One night Tony talked about Fiona Beecham, some girl Jason couldn't even remember. Apparently they both went to primary school with her. Then Tony said she'd teased him all the way through grade three, and Jason remembered her.

'She was a horror head … and she wasn't the only one …'

He saw Tony looking at him through his red eyes.

'The only horror head?'

'No, ya tool. She wasn't the only one teasing you.'

Jason threw him another bag of corn chips. Tony opened them up and asked, 'Do you think you'll ever get married?'

'To *you*? Nope.'

Tony looked at him and grinned. Waiting for more *deep and mournful*, Jason figured.

'Nah, too fucken expensive.'

Tony didn't smile and Jason felt his eyes on him.

'Do you think you ever will, Jase?'

Jason shook his head; there was no pleasing the boy.

'I spose, if I find the right chick … probly.'

'You still seeing Karen from Just Jeans?' Tony asks.

'No … that's, nah … that's all over. She wanted to move.'

'To Melbourne?'

Jason kept watching the video, a band dousing themselves with paint.

'Anywhere,' he told him. 'She didn't care.'

Guitars thrummed and the scene cut to a girl in black lingerie.

'Don't think I'll ever get married.'

Jason laughed. 'Don't say that, mate. You've got your blow-up doll. Wadda ya call her?'

Tony didn't say anything more for a while, then he started talking about Essendon and whether they'd make the finals. Soon he was snoring in his beanbag so Jason turned off the TV and left.

Jason walks across McPherson's two paddocks every morning now. By the time he reaches the skip, the dew has darkened his fading black boots. If Shell doesn't get a replacement for Tony soon he reckons he might have to buy a special pair of 'work' gumboots. Another twenty bucks gone.

At least they've got Peter what's-his-name to cover the nightshift. So Jason just has to handle the couple of busy patches during the day. Early in the morning a few trucks come through, then there's the after-school rush. The rest of the time there's a steady trickle of cars and trucks for quick petrol and Mars bars before they race on.

Jason looks out from the console desk into the growing darkness and the Hume Highway. The top of a truck goes past, a muffled scream from its motor as it powers south to Melbourne.

Where the chicks are.

The rumour's stronger than the blow-up doll, but no

one laughs when they tell each other this one: Tony organ-
ised a Filipino bride, but she saw a picture of him and
decided not to come. He couldn't face telling his mum, *No,
actually, I won't be getting married now.*

Tony probably sat here at the counter writing letters to
the village girl, grinning at his reflection in the window as
the day darkened. He was probably making secret trips to
Bendigo or somewhere, trying to get a suit to fit. Jason
smiles to himself and then gets a tightness in his guts and
neck, the same one he gets every time he thinks of Tony.
The driveway is empty so he heads out to the skip for a
smoke.

The sun's leaving its orange peel everywhere and he
looks at the emerging stars, the tip of Mount Twyford
pushing up as if it might have something to say to them. All
around the base of the mountain there are fires, farmers
burning off. One of the blazes is bigger than the others and
the smoke is heading right up to the mountain peak and
the stars that are getting brighter every minute.

Back at the console, Jason flicks through the newspaper.
For a joke he's been looking at the personals most days:
guy seeks guy – he laughs; mature woman wants younger
man. He looks through the Murchville and Bendigo
columns. Sometimes even Melbourne: girl seeks guy, 30+
for fun times.

'And maybe kids and a mortgage,' Jason says, and closes
the paper. Then he opens it again and takes another look at
the Melbourne column. He's still looking and munching a
donut when Pete walks in.

Cappuccino, Soft Drink
and the End of the World

From the day we moved into our high-rise apartment, I was listening for them. I hardly noticed them at first; they weren't as loud. And they were just new things among many. But after a few months I heard a noise while I was in bed with Andrew, a sudden deep thump that didn't sound like thunder.

'What was that?' I asked.

'I don't know.'

'Something in the Docklands?' I said to him and the dark bedroom.

I waited for him to answer, but he rustled the sheets and turned over.

In the silence that followed I could hear him breathing. Was he listening to hear if it would come again? Was he wondering, like I was, if the noise came from the middle of the earth or somewhere in the sky?

Last night I sat on our couch, staring at the pen and blank sheet of paper on the coffee table.

When the deep pounding started, it seemed to be the noise of cargo containers dropped by forklifts in the Docklands, somewhere way below our apartment. But then the sounds became difficult to distinguish. They seemed louder than wharf activity should be, closer than sounds that big could possibly be. They echoed along unseen tunnels somewhere below us. Or were they above us?

I jumped every time I heard the sound, but Andrew was more relaxed. He seemed not to notice them as much. Or I thought he was pretending not to, so I could be the 'paranoid one' and he the 'casual one'. Either way he kept his eyes fixed on his magazine.

I decided to make some phone calls.

'You say it's a loud, booming sound, but sometimes *not* a boom?' the gruff voice said.

'Yes, that's right . . .'

'Well, look, I don't mean to be rude, but have you had your hearing tested?'

'No. My hearing's fine . . . thanks.'

Idiot.

No matter what the building warden or anyone else thought, to me those sounds were organic – amplified heartbeats come loose from a hospital monitor, flowing out into the night. They were noises for which, I thought, our ears were made. Sounds the world might make if it was ending. Or perhaps becoming something new.

When I met Andrew I was lead worship singer at Carnegie Christian Fellowship. I wore my hair longer and parted it slightly to the side. People find it hard to believe until I show them the photos. Every Sunday I was behind the microphone, voice pitched high, eyes closed, head raised to heaven – a zone somewhere beyond the rafters of a hired school gymnasium.

During an after-service morning tea, he manoeuvred past the three or four people ringed around me.

'Wow, you've got an amazing voice.'

I smiled and was about to tell him my name.

'My name's Andrew,' he chipped in. 'I've been coming here a few weeks.'

He put his coffee mug down on a trestle table, extended his hand and smiled. I liked his goatee beard; I could never grow one thick enough, and it annoyed my wife when we kissed.

'Bless you, brother. My name's David McConachy.'

It was 1991, the beginning of the Gulf War. Each night on TV, Janine and I watched the green lights of Armageddon over Baghdad. The round-the-clock coverage had us reaching for our 'end-time' books by Christian authors. The books seemed to be saying the prophesied time could be upon us: the Anti-Christ, a master of politics and illusion, might soon appear to solve the world's problems – in exchange for global worship.

We watched gas-masked journalists reporting from Israel's border, looking out across thousands of kilometres of desert to where Iraq's missiles were aimed at the Holy Land. We kept our eyes fixed on the screen, speaking without looking at each other, dipping Tim Tams into instant coffee. We thought of our children asleep upstairs in the glow of pink teddy-bear lamps – were their souls known by the Lord, *truly*? Were they – and *we* – ready for the Anti-Christ's reign to begin? While I watched scientists discuss the power of a Scud missile, Janine would often go to bed early. She had to get up for work, she said.

'Unless the world is going to end tonight,' she'd sometimes grin, 'and then I'll likely get the day off.'

I didn't take my eyes off the TV.

Before I met Andrew, I hadn't come across an eschatologist as fervent as me. But he made my end-time scenarios look as simple as Sunday School songs. He knew all my theories, several adaptations of them, and more. He had his own prophecies.

'There will be a fire in the city of Babylon, which can only be Baghdad ... All the believers will be caught up in the air after the sign has been seen by all the earth ... The return of Jesus seems likely to occur between August 1992 and June 1993, according to Daniel 7:16 and the following verses from Revelation ...'

His mouth must have moved when he spoke, but it seemed instead that parchments were unravelling from his chest. I spent every Sunday afternoon and evening with Andrew. With Janine – when she wasn't in the bedroom with the kids – and twelve others from church, we drank cappuccino and soft drink and talked about the end of the world. Around the table all eyes were on Andrew. Words flowed from him at a catastrophic rate. I took notes and others followed my lead.

The Sunday meetings turned to regular weeknight

gatherings that soon became every night of the week. In our living room, biscuits on a plate and several Bibles on the table, we contemplated whether or not we should flee to the country and take the true believers from our church with us. Somewhere in the countryside we could build a base and stock it with tinned food and fallout-survival gear. We'd have the opportunity then, after we were cut off from the economic system, to evangelise as many people as possible. Save them from the coming bombs, the fire and judgement.

But then the Gulf War ended, and after a few weeks the numbers in our group diminished. It became just Andrew and me. We remained convinced – Andrew was certain – the end was coming.

To Sunday meetings at the cafe we added picnics and prayer walks along the beach at Elwood. Then we made weekend-long reconnaissance trips to the country to pray about where we should be, both spiritually and geographically, when the end came upon us.

When I first held Andrew's hand it seemed like I'd done it for a long time. We walked palm-upon-palm along a secluded Daylesford trail and the birds *thip thipped* in the bushes, diving to unseen nests. The rain was so light it almost didn't fall on our shoulders. I looked across at Andrew and it seemed I'd lost a centimetre or two from my height. Where his eyes had been level with mine, weren't they now just a little higher? His smile was still the same, but no words left his mouth, no prophesies, no warnings. His mouth upon mine.

Several Sundays we enjoyed lunch outdoors at The Boathouse restaurant, looking out over the blue and shining lake. One afternoon, I took small sips of white wine and watched the glint on the water.

'Do you think this lake is a crater, from a meteor?'

Andrew huffed, smiled and shook his head a little. He spoke gently. 'No, David. No, it's man-made.'

In less than a year my church worship ministry was over, along with my marriage and family life. After ten years serving the church I was expelled, Andrew along with me.

A friend who also left the church some months after we did wrote me a letter – even then, it appeared, to meet was out of the question. He said the 'scandal' was never spoken about, officially. Yet it was always spoken about. Not my name or Andrew's, only words that describe what happens when the wicked come amongst the pure and deceive them: *Thorns. Choking. Seed on barren ground. The serpent, the lies . . .*

Sitting on the couch last night the pen finally reached my hand, unsteady as my stomach, turning over itself. The piece of paper remained blank on the steel coffee table.

A few years before, I had written and written. Notes from conversations with Andrew. They were his lectures, I suppose. And those notes became journals, packed with spiritual insights and ideas, theories about the end of the world. In America today there are Christian novels on the bestseller lists, all about the end of the world. I could have written one. Or ten.

Maybe not ten. The material dried up quickly after we moved into the apartment.

I loved the sound of his voice when he talked about the end of the world. But in the clubs, when we talked at all, it was spirits, pills and the start of a new world. I suppose you can't talk about the end, can you, when you're a soldier in the very force that's tearing apart the family unit, the church, all the *godly*, all the *righteous* . . .

Technically – *Christianly* – speaking, the new life Andrew and I had together was an 'old' life, a life that should have been left behind when we were 'born again'. I'd grown up in a church family with a fire-breathing preacher for a father; I'd never before lived anything like this kind of life. But Andrew knew how to live it in the same detail he'd known about the end of the world. It was a life where our leg hairs rubbed together under white linen, little tablets brought us visions from who could really say where now? I used to sway when I led worship at church, but I'd never really danced. For a while I liked the nightclub lights on my head as I tried to find some moves. Andrew usually danced on a different part of the floor.

September 11 came and went and I can guess what our church was like: sermons on the terror of Islam, songs proclaiming the coming of the Holy City of Jerusalem from the sky . . . Then Melbourne was promised a spate of terrorism, but the only things Andrew and I spoke about were share prices, property and the need to invest in gold. Even the noises in the night were off the agenda.

'Look, *what* sounds? Go to sleep, will you . . .'

Terrorism. The Middle East in crisis. I wanted to hold him, be held. Or fight. Do anything. But I fought the bedclothes and pleaded silently for sleep to come before the thumping started up again.

One night he took pity on me. He got up and made us both some coffee. He even smiled.

'You can't sleep and you won't let me, so why not make it worse?'

We drank half the coffee, he took off his white robe and he made love to me.

Afterward he raised the blind and we sat on the edge of the bed. I looked out over the bay at the silver blinking lights and the grim orange of a city sky that never seemed to find a home in darkness.

'What *is* it? Do you miss your wife . . . Is it the *kids*? The access stuff again?'

I looked at the side of his face and spoke quickly. But honestly.

'No. It's not that . . .'

I looked down into the blackness of my cold coffee. I felt Andrew's presence in front of me, waiting for my answer, but I couldn't find any words. When I looked up, his naked body was heading into the en suite, swooshing the sliding door closed behind him. I whispered, 'I miss *you*.' Then the shower hissed to life and Andrew started singing.

He came out in a white towel and he was about to speak when there was a loud thump. It echoed like something inside a ship, like a shout inside a whale. Rifling through the underwear drawer, Andrew seemed to pause for a moment. I stared at him and half smiled. He couldn't pretend to have not heard it. But he stared back at me, his eyes wide.

'What?'

I shook my head and looked away from him, out the window at the dark sea and docks below.

I had the pen in my mouth, chewing it – wrong end and I could taste ink. I wondered whether I should try writing on a laptop. Print out whatever it was I wanted to say and stick it on our bedroom door. I could 'borrow' Andrew's computer again.

Every night for the last month he'd sat cross-legged on the couch, hunched over his laptop while he thought I was asleep. From the doorway I could see the back of his head, the nape of his neck in the lamp light.

Night after night I let it go on – I suppose I hoped it would stop. But at the same time I somehow knew it wouldn't. Finally, I queried him.

'What am I *doing*?' he said, then sniggered. He later claimed he hadn't.

'Yes, what are you doing, typing every night?'

'It's none of your business . . .'

I didn't step away. I stood silent.

'David,' he said, using his mushy voice. 'It's just some *work* I have to do at home . . .'

'Let me see it.'

'You're being ridiculous.'

'Let me see it!'

He showed me the screen. Some purple and green graphs.

'They don't take much typing . . .'

He smiled.

'It's not the only thing I'm working on . . .'

He didn't need to convince me of *that*. And on the bottom of the page the graphs were dated 1998.

He looked up at me and smiled. I stared at him, but didn't speak.

'Oooh, angry . . .'

I went to the bedroom and a few minutes later I heard him typing again.

He went out one night and over the phone a friend helped me crack his password. I broke into his Sent Mail folder.

He was out again last night, working overtime. I'm sure he was working overtime. Talking again, no doubt. I suppose it takes a while to set things in motion; it took *us* two years. And I'd wonder what they talked about if I didn't already know: movies. Suddenly Andrew knows all about the movies.

The last three nights the sounds were the loudest I'd

heard and no one could possibly sleep through them. But Andrew only shuffled in his sleep and drew in some breath while I lay terrified.

Were they sonic booms? Buildings falling? Missiles hurled into the docks?

I put the pen down and rested my hands on my chin. I looked out the apartment window, down into the watery darkness. White lights were bubbling across the bay. Beyond those lights there would be others I couldn't see shining in towns, and beyond them cities and the lights on airport runways. I watched the red blinking of a plane in the black sky, disappearing only to be replaced a few seconds later by another. One of them could take me off the ground and set me down again in a city with the same lights as Melbourne, but ruled by a different language.

The sounds that had built up so much in the last three days were all over me. They pumped along my arms, through my chest, into my head and down into parts of me I couldn't name and that seemed to have no role in the transfer of blood to my organs. Those sounds were everywhere inside me and somehow outside me as well. They filled up my senses and the world that senses draw from; I knew there was nowhere I could be where they weren't. The sounds that had been threatening and dangerous for so long were becoming a comfort. I knew they were meant for me. And only for me.

From the shelf I picked up a frame and looked at the photo: Andrew and me sitting at an *el fresco* table in Oxford Street during one of our trips to Sydney. His hair was

longer then, brown and blond layers. I smiled when I realised that, even though I knew they were under those layers,
fleshy and delectable at the lobe, I was checking to see if
Andrew had ears.

I picked up the pen and it felt loose and free in my hand:
Andrew, this is the end for us . . .

Driven from Darackmore to Toonenbuck

There were rumours all around Darackmore last night that unmarked police cars had screamed into Toonenbuck. Big, dark Commodores all the way from Melbourne. I was out for a girls' night so I heard all about it. But John didn't cos he was at home watching the footy.

I couldn't hide the *Sunday Herald Sun* from him this morning, though.

He sat at the table, staring at page three. His spoon was in his cereal, but he didn't dig anything out. He just looked down at the paper. I put my hand on his shoulder and he stayed sitting there for a bit. Then he was up and out the back sliding door. Now he's just sitting there on the kids' swing, lighting up a smoke. He's puffing smoke out and swinging back and forward a bit. He's got his shorts on. I like him in those. His legs don't look much different to when I met him in high school. I reckon it was a day when he was wearing his blue school shorts that I decided I'd marry him. Or at least have his babies.

I was born in Darackmore and so was John. He lived on a farm, five kays out near Patterson but still, between us, we've lived in the area all our lives. Except for when we went to live in Heathmere for two years so John could play footy with them. He got paid, but not enough, far as I was concerned, to keep us two hours trip away from our families. They said they'd give him more money to stay for another year, but I'm glad we came back.

John's had the Mobil servo for about ten years now. He's always been a car man. Reckons when he was five his dad showed him the ins and outs of an engine. Shone the torch all over an old HQ's motor, pointing out the head gasket, plugs, the fan. Wasn't much else in them, John told me.

Every now and again he gets it in his head that he wants to pack up the tools and do something else. Says he's sick of working on late-model cars. What the hell else does he reckon he's gunna do? I remind him about the years he did in Bonlac's factory before he became a registered mechanic. Does he want to go back to the stink of cheesy, milky crap spewing into vats all day? That usually shuts him up. Plus, I remind him the good thing about working on late-model cars: no one's too cluey about how they work. He can charge a fair whack to do stuff that he hasn't got much idea about cos no one else has got a clue either.

Enough said. John's cheaper than any bastard in Melbourne and he doesn't get many complaints.

I put me bowl in the dishwasher and stick a couple of bits of bread in the toaster. I look out the glass sliding door again and John's looking up at me, all sad eyes. I pull me dressing gown tight around me and head outside.

'It's not *your* bloody fault.'

He looks up at me. 'Keep ya voice down.'

He gets off the swing and walks over to the washing line. Looks at it like there's something more important than his overalls hanging there.

'It's Sunday mornin, Johnny. No one's gunna hear us.'

'There's always someone around.'

I head back inside to get him the toast.

Darackmore's not a big place. Last census we came in at 2512. But Sandra Mulligan at the council reckons they buggerise around with those numbers so we can keep our 'town status'. Dunno what that's all about. It's still a town as far as I can tell, no matter how many people live in it.

We're much bigger than Patterson and Mortdale though, and definitely Toonenbuck. I don't think there's fifty people out there these days. The Bramsoke Council wanted to push the speed limit through the place back up to one hundred kays. Only the Crown Hotel car park stopped them. Tom Sheppard the publican got stuck into the council one night and said his 'patrons' could get wiped out pulling into traffic from the car park.

Apparently George Sinclair from the council yelled out, 'That's if they haven't been wiped out by your mob already.'

A few of the others had a snigger. Tom wasn't impressed by all reports. Stared at them all till they quietened down.

Threatened to get his cousin from Melbourne to look into it all. The one that has 'a few different ventures'. That worried em. Plus his cronies were sitting alongside Sheppard with their fat heads and arms covered in tatts.

I don't reckon Sheppard and his mob have done as many things as everyone's said over the years. If they have, Christ knows why they're still free to lean all over the Crown bar every night. John reckons for sure they did what they were supposed to have done to Chris Harrison's eye. The poor bastard wears a patch now. Said it was a stuff up with fencing wire flinging back at him, but John tells me that's bullshit.

Still, it's eighty kays an hour through Toonenbuck and past the Crown, but you've gotta do sixty clicks through Darackmore. You've got the Avenue of Honour, pine trees on your left and right. If you're coming from Melbourne way, the bluestone Catholic Church comes up on your left, and the school next door to it. About a half a kay on there's Maccas on your right, houses on both sides and the Three Maids Hotel. You go past all the other shops, then there's another school, the Anglican Church and then John's Mobil out where there aren't as many houses. During the day there's usually a car up on a hoist and John there with his head up under it.

If you drove through Darack last Friday night, though, you wouldn't have seen much of all that because the street-lights're shithouse. But the Mobil garage light was on and John was in there still with his head up under a car. John should've told whoever's car it was to get stuffed cos he had a party to go to. But he's got a bad habit of trying to make everything sweet with everyone. That's why he's out there now on the swing, worrying.

Seven a clock he rings me and says the car's timing's all stuffed up and he'll probably be another couple of hours. I told him you're not bloody wrong the timing's all stuffed up, what about the party tonight? John said just get the babysitter to come a bit later and he'd get home as soon as he could.

I go out to the swing and give him a couple of peanut butter toasts. He asks where the kids are and I tell him Brent's still in bed and the other two are watching a DVD. He takes a bite out of one of his toasts and then looks up at me.

'I've gotta go down the station and tell em what I know.' He swallows then takes another bite.

I shake my head at him.

'You're not goin anywhere. What can you tell em, anyway?'

'Tell em I could've done somethin.'

I sigh at him.

'Like what? That's bullshit, John.'

He grabs tighter on the swing rope like he's going to pull himself up and head off. I get worried he might be serious.

'Look, just sit there for a bit, will ya? Have a think about it. I'll go and make you a cuppa.'

I put my hand on his shoulder and he looks down again at his toast.

We'd been at the party for half an hour. John was sitting at an outdoor table, looking at his stubby. I said to him, 'What's the matter with you? You're quiet . . .'

So he spilled his guts. What there was to spill.

He reckons he knew straight away they were from out of town. Even before he heard the tins rattling along behind their car and saw 'Just Married' scrawled in white paint on a side panel. A bloke with darkish skin wound down his window. John said the woman leaning across from the passenger seat had a kind of, but not really, Asian-looking face.

He told them, 'Pump's closed, sorry.'

The bloke said, 'No, not, not, we stay . . .'

John was gunna give him a blast, but then he realised the bloke was looking for somewhere to stay the night. He gave him directions back into town: past the school on your left, the second big pine tree, to the sign that says 500 metres, the river alongside you, then you're at Fenwick Guesthouse.

'It'll have a vacancy,' he said. 'Everything else is probably full up. Footy finals and the flower show, ya know.'

John reckons the bloke looked at him dumb-like and the woman sniffed and blew her nose.

Playing the tour guide wasn't getting the car in the garage fixed or John any closer to getting home for a shower and spruce up. He tried again to explain how to get to the Fenwick, but the pair of them came out with a heap of 'whos' and 'whats' all in the wrong order so John said, 'Toonenbuck.'

He pointed straight down the highway, talked them

through the right over the bridge that you couldn't miss, and then straight on to the Crown Hotel. They'd have a bed. The woman smiled, the bloke said, 'We thank', shoved ten bucks in John's hand and they pulled away.

John reckons straight away he felt his guts sink. Just the thought of this pair bowling up to Sheppard and his mob at the Crown. On a Friday night. Didn't like it one iota so he waved his hand and they pulled up. He ran up to the bloke's side and the bloke wound down his window. Not as far this time.

'Mate, look, I'll grab me car and show ya the way to the Fenwick.'

John tried to shove the ten bucks back into the bloke's hand.

The bloke said, 'No, no, you keep.' The woman smiled and they pulled away, tin cans rattling down the highway behind their Nissan Bluebird.

I've boiled the kettle twice. Put a couple of last night's pizza plates in the dishwasher, keeping me eyes on John the whole time. I'm watching him when he's up and off the swing and in through the back sliding door. Straight past me and grabbing the car keys off the hook.

'Where ya goin, John?'

He looks at me, but he's still clammed up and heading for the front door. I go after him and we both end up on the front decking. I grab his arm and it stops him.

'Just stay put. You didn't do anything.'

With his free arm he grabs me, then talks through his teeth like he's some tough bloke.

'If I didn't do anythin then it doesn't matter if I go down and tell em what I know . . .'

I raise me voice and that gets him looking from one neighbour's yard to the other.

'For Chrissake, John! You've worked bloody hard to keep the servo goin and you've got three kids. You don't want to go and get mixed up in all that stuff at Toonenbuck.'

He goes to pull his arm away when we both see the dark-coloured Commodores drive past, and a normal cop car behind them. There's blokes in suits with dark sunnies on, sitting in all the Commodores. I reckon I catch a look at a couple of the regulars from the Crown in the backseat of one of them. I ask John whether he thinks it is and he says he doesn't know.

'It's alright now,' I say, but John just keeps looking at the cars.

We stand there and watch them speed up as they hit the eighty-zone. When the last one disappears over the rise, I head back inside. But John doesn't.

I come back out and bring him a cup of tea and sit down next to him on the edge of the decking. He sits there and blows his smoke out, looking away toward the rise in the road. I put my arm around him.

That Bali Smile

I didn't want to go out that night, to the Sari Club or anywhere else. If the truth were known, which it so often isn't, I probably shouldn't have been in Bali at all. It's really not my kind of place for a holiday. I like cultural experiences and getting to know what happens in the lives of ordinary people in a country. If I was organising my own budget holiday, I would have gone to Vietnam.

But I'm not totally averse to nightlife, and Bali has got plenty of it. It's just that, usually, I like things quieter, lower key. Places you can talk. Not necessarily in lounge chairs, but definitely in booths, with light jazz playing. Perhaps candles on the table and men who can rouse me out of myself, my thought-life. But they're so rare. Before that holiday, I'd spent five years hanging around with either unattractive men who were, at least, great conversationalists, or attractive men who turned out to be Peter Pans.

I'd been working long hours in the research department and my sister, who has more money than she has ideas about what to do with it, decided she would pay for my trip.

'It'll be great, Rache,' she said, smiling because she knows I prefer 'Rachel'. 'You'll love it: cute guys, cheap food, clothes, DVDs – cheap beer!'

I don't drink beer. But in the end I couldn't resist a free holiday, even if it was with her advertising-exec friends. If nothing else they make great anthropology. They give me faces to put on statistics I read about our culture's shift from communitarian principles to atomised, individualistic and situational values. As long as I used only short words and read thin books when we sunbaked around the pool, the girls tolerated me. Even if they couldn't understand why, instead of running with them for the safety of the hotel and the pool, I bothered chatting with the hoards of smiling Balinese selling fake watches and perfume in the street.

I was sunburnt that night, red across my white shoulders because I'd kept reading, sprawled out near the pool on a plastic lounge chair, when I should have been dashing up to my hotel room for sunscreen. And I'm sure I had a touch of Bali belly coming on; my stomach felt airy and kept turning over itself.

But my sister talked me into going out.

'C'mon, Rache, you'll be okay ... couple of G&Ts and you'll be anyone's,' she laughed.

Maybe I drank a lot that night because of my stomach – the sense that if I filled it with liquid the airiness would disappear. And it did. But Bali belly disappears at night anyway. That's what Heath said and I had no reason to disbelieve him.

Heath knew Bali. He knew lots of interesting facts about so many countries and their histories. And not just mindless facts, either. He knew when American presidents had signed treaties in the twentieth century and what those treaties had meant for the world's cultural and economic situation. Yes, he was a financial consultant, formerly an economist, but he loved historical studies and biographies. He loved *lives*. He looked at me across the table and smiled like I had something of his in my bag and was only keeping it from him for fun.

He had a gorgeous slant to his muscular body, leaning to the left as he danced, brown arms emerging from a white t-shirt. I didn't dance very often and I could feel the girls' smiles all over me. Heath smiled, too; a beautiful smile, beautiful teeth. I felt my body freeing up, my legs doing whatever they wanted to, ignoring my brain. Heath smiled again, leant his body into the pugnacious music and spoke words in my ear that I couldn't catch.

I grinned and craned my head up toward his ear to say I hadn't heard what he'd said. He was taking a light grip on my hand when the white flash came and then the explosion.

A few minutes that felt like days later I was lying on my back on the street. There was screaming and shouting and sirens in the hot air that I was breathing in but wanting to spit out.

How does the brain work? Does it retain the last information before a shock, or was it the shock itself that made me, as soon as I could move, go looking for Heath and not my sister, ignoring the seeping wetness on my legs and the pain in my shoulder?

My body limped past dead people, some with missing

limbs and torn clothing. They were in my line of vision, but I didn't really see them. There were voices like sirens and then the sirens themselves. When I heard the second explosion I thought I was just remembering the first – the seething panic was drowned out for a moment. I didn't crouch or cover my head. People swung through the air as if thrown from a grotesque merry-go-round, metal and glass accompanying rag-doll flights. My eyes wanted to close but I couldn't make them. Something hard hit my uninjured arm and I fell to my knees, but then I saw Heath lying face down ten metres away.

I looked at his motionless body and immediately thought of spinal fracture. I wondered if I should turn him over when I heard a musical sound, very faint below the yelling and sirens, and I realised that his mobile was ringing in his jeans pocket.

My husband was a wonderful, wonderful man. He drove me to my office every day and then picked me up when he finished work. He often finished work early or brought work home just so he could be in time to pick me up and we could be together for the evening commute. And he always, no matter how stressful the day had been for him, had a smile for me.

I know, I'm *sure*, that sometimes he didn't smile all day until he saw me. And I know that sometimes he didn't really even want to be smiling then. But his smile was just his way of telling me not to worry about him.

A few weeks before his business trip to Indonesia, he put his briefcase down on the kitchen bench and sighed. I heard him. He denied it, but I heard him. I watched him head upstairs to the shower. I didn't follow. He wanted to be alone, I'm sure. He always did when he was feeling low. He liked solitude a lot of the time, actually. I wouldn't say he liked it more than spending time with me, but he did spend a lot of nights reading those biographies and history books. I could have blamed all that reading for why we never got around to having kids! He would have been a wonderful, wonderful father.

In bed that night I said, 'Heath, you can tell me how you feel.'

'Yes, I know. I know I can, Meagan. But why bring you down, too?'

I suggested the holiday. Why not stopover in Bali after your last meeting in Jakarta? He thought perhaps five days. I was a bit shocked and wondered whether two might be better. We decided on three. I should have insisted that he made it two. But I've given up the what-ifs.

That's a lie. You never give up the what-ifs.

There's no doubt he needed to unwind, needed to get his smile back for himself, not just me. He didn't ring much while he was on the trip, so I suppose he was entertaining a lot of clients. I'm sure they dragged him along to the Sari Club. He didn't like all that music and dancing.

When his father took a turn for the worse, his mother asked if I would call Heath for her. I didn't really want to ring, not because I thought she should do it, though.

I mean, she was at her husband's bedside day and night. No, it was because I didn't want to disturb Heath again on his holiday. He'd sounded a little tense when I'd rung him that morning. He said he was coming back the next day so there was no need for me to call. But I could still hear a smile in his voice.

So even though I was reluctant, I thought he'd want to know straight away that his dad had gone into hospital again.

I was listening to Heath's mobile ringing and looking at the blood running from what remained of his right leg and somehow my sight and hearing were connected to the sounds of sirens and people screaming and running around me. There was a smell in the air that I hadn't noticed before in Bali, not even rising from a street vendor's wok.

A man was turning Heath over, and then he stopped. Was he a doctor? He moved down the street and crouched beside a woman, touched her arm. Another woman ran past, in a tight pink skirt, screaming, 'Where are you, Steve? Where are you, Steve?' over and over. I turned Heath from his side onto his back. His eyes were closed and his face was black in patches, but his teeth were still white.

When I danced with him, I looked into Heath's face and imagined us living in an apartment, perhaps one with a view of the city or maybe a parkland. I had these pre-bedroom fantasies – a happy-ever-after life of smiles across cafe tables, the baby capsule at our feet – whenever I started to think I might go against my perennial better judgement and sleep with a guy on a whim. With that in mind I could enjoy him inside me and it would feel like forever.

That night we would have been *one*. It was that simple. We would have been one, dreaming together of being more, and that was worth vodkas and gin and drunken sex. One night. *That* night. A night that was forever and a perfect smile. That dance floor and its music that sounded like a war in progress and how was I, or any of us, to know that we were in the middle of one? And we were dancing. I looked at Heath on the ground and I actually thought it: He won't be dancing anymore.

Somewhere the rest of his leg had merged into the humid and screaming night. I looked at him. I didn't try to figure out if he was alive, dead, breathing or unconscious. I sat and looked at his face, listened to his phone. It stopped ringing.

Even lying there he looked sexy.

His phone rang again.

When I rang him, I had no idea, no idea at all that the Sari Club had been bombed. I didn't find out until after I had made both calls. I don't know much about mobile phones, but I've since found out that the call was hung up.

Heath's phone was found at the bomb scene, not with his body, so it must have been on a table in the nightclub and it just went flying out of there with everything else in the explosion. The mobile was kept for a short time by the

Federal Police, then given to me. I keep it now with Heath's ashes on the shelf of my walk-in-robes.

Someone who heard his phone ringing in the wreckage must have grabbed it and then hung up. Of course they hung up – what is a person in a life-threatening situation, in the middle of a bombed-out nightclub, going to say to a stranger on the end of a mobile phone? Or maybe the phone was stepped on by an emergency worker, causing it to hang up.

It doesn't matter. Heath didn't answer.

They say his leg was crushed by debris, but they're not sure if it was in the first or second blast. It's my hunch it was the second. I can see him, after the first explosion, one of the few who went back in to help others escape, dragging bodies from the wreckage, through the smoke and confusion. He would have been there, in the fire and the collapsing beams from the nightclub, as diligently as he came to collect me from work every night, searching for someone to pick up, lift out of the charcoal and broken glass and carry to the safety of an ambulance, someone whose life he could save. He loved reading all those biographies, especially finding out how one little event, someone making a change of plans and being there at the right moment for someone else, how that could turn another person's life around.

I've got no doubt that Heath, who hated bars and nightclubs, who only went to them to please his clients, was at the Sari Club for a reason, that he saved someone's life, that someone has him to thank for being alive right now.

He was a wonderful, wonderful man.

Why did I do it? Was it because we had no future and I thought I might like to talk to his past, his present? Get as close to him as I could? I took the phone out of his pocket. I tried not to think it, but I did: I like the feeling of my hand in there.

There was a name on the screen: Meagan. I could have picked up the call:

Hello, Meagan.

Who's this?

My name's Rachel.

Rachel? Who are you? Where's Heath?

Heath's here. He's with me.

Meagan's voice would have started to wobble.

Why? What's going on?

There's been an explosion. Two people meeting. There's nothing you can do about it. I'm sorry, Meagan, but Heath's with me.

Silence on the line. Meagan wouldn't know what to say, up against a woman who had just found what she wanted and wouldn't let go.

I . . . what are . . .

Meagan, don't worry. He's happy. He's dancing with me. You should see him. He moves beautifully, gracefully.

Through the steps of divorce, re-marriage and setting up a new home.

I let the phone continue to ring.

The ambulance officers arrived and I thought, This is one of the first times I've seen Balinese men without smiles on their faces. One of them raised Heath's arm and took his pulse. He looked at his partner and they both gave quick shakes of their heads and one of them looked at me.

The phone was still ringing. Meagan's name. I rejected the call.

They put Heath's body on a stretcher. Before they covered his face with a white sheet, I looked at it, bent down to him. I know I was looking for something, but I couldn't think what it was.

Each officer grabbed an end of the stretcher and lifted.

'He your husband?'

I didn't answer. The ambulance officer carried Heath away.

Talisman

Dad was the best footy player the district had ever seen, forget the rest. They reckon he could do anything on a footy field. Could have played in the VFL, easy, would have starred, but he didn't want to leave Leongatha. I never got to see him play, or if I did I was too young to remember.

My brothers saw him. Mick said one day Dad stood like a sailor on Leon McLaughlin's shoulders – the bloke who ended up playing basketball in Melbourne – and took a speccy. You get a few blokes together in any front bar of any pub in Gippsland and if they drink for long enough they'll start talking about that mark.

Dad's mates had more stories than just the one about the mark though. They told as many as they could whenever they came over, which was almost every night once they heard things were going belly-up at the farm.

Brian and Mick sent me out plenty of nights to listen to them. That was the usual visitor policy – send out the youngest to spy on the adults. I would creep down the hallway and then come to the thin strip of light shining on the carpet and look into the lounge. Most nights Mum'd be alone in the lounge room, watching *Prisoner* or some other show, drinking tea, the heater making her face glow orange.

But one night I watched Dad's mates drink with him in that little room just off the lounge room, the one with the record player in it and most of Dad's trophies. I saw Peter O'Neil point at the little replicas of the '72 and '73 premiership cups and remind Dad that he'd run up the street in the nude the nights they'd won the flags.

'You were on a roll, Doug.'

'Yeah, and now it's all bloody downhill.'

Dad was smiling, but his eyes were different. Kind of like paddocks the way they fill up slowly with rain on a really wet day.

'Now I can't even keep the fucken wolves from the door.'

Even though as far as she knew there were no kids up, Mum still called out from the lounge, 'Keep your language down.' Dad didn't joke to his mates or say anything back to Mum. He just sat there looking at the backs of his hands folded together as if there was something important written on them he was trying to read.

When I head off for school in the mornings, I walk across the lawn and look behind me to where Dad's ute's parked in the garage. Walking down the dirt track to the highway, I look through the gaps in the pine trees and I can see him in the paddocks on his quadbike, the thick wheels climbing the rises.

Then two mornings in a row the garage is empty. The third night my brothers wake me up and send me down the corridor. They've heard a car door slam. I peer into the gap between the lounge-room door and its frame, just below the hinges.

'You're completely useless. Get outta my house!' Mum says.

'*Your* house? You wooden have a house if it wasn't for me slavin me guts out with those fuggen cows . . .'

Dad's face is red and his words are all out of shape like your hair when you get up in the morning.

'Zit my fault about deregulation? The fuggen prices have dropped, what can I do? Zit my fault the rotary fugged up and the new one's buggered? My fault half the cows are crook? Geesuz . . .'

Mum eyeballs him.

'Maybe if you spent more time sorting out the stuff-ups and less time at the pub with your bloody mates re-livin the glory days we wouldn't be in the mess we're in!'

'Ah get fugged.'

And Dad's heading out of the lounge room toward the door crack I've got my eye stuck to so I'm off down the corridor, running but trying not to let my feet touch the ground.

'What are you doing out of bed you little bastard?' Dad's after me down the corridor but I'm through my bedroom door and under my bed, right up in the corner against the wall where he'd have to squat right down and reach in to get hold of me. I'm banking on him not doing that with his back being a bit crook these days.

'Get outta there, Stevie. I'll give ya bloody hidin . . . up at this time, whattaya playin at?'

I stay quiet, breathing into the wall. He's not bending down, looks like I've got out of it.

'Right, fella, that's it. You're goin to town with me tomorra.'

I haven't got out of it.

I hated trips into town more than helping Mum hang out the huge white sheets and getting tangled up in them, more than helping hose out the dairy and getting cow poo stuck, all green sometimes and mushy, onto my gumboots.

I spend the half-hour drive into town watching everyone's paddocks go past. We pull up at Dalgety's first, the clouds looking dark, but I follow Dad who's wearing a black beanie. I'm wearing my Bombers one. If it was raining, I'd have to sit in the ute because Dad didn't want me getting wet hopping in and out.

'Still can't get that lad to barrack for a decent team, Doug?'

It's Keith Chambers in his pale-blue Dalgety's shirt, with his silver hair and mo and big chest. He used to coach Dad. They both barrack for Collingwood.

'Nah, he's a bloody drongo ... can't keep him out of the library either, mate. Fillin his head with all kinds of rubbish. Too bloody clever for his boots ...'

Dad looks down at me and there's something a bit like a smile in the corner of his mouth but it's kind of crooked, like his mouth is a set of handlebars someone is trying to bend into shape after a stack.

Keith Chambers walks out from behind the counter and Dad follows him to the back of the shop. While they look over dairy rotary parts, Dad tells me to nick off for a bit and I try to be interested in the orange sheep-dip backpacks in the row behind them.

'Still doin it tough?'

'Keep your voice down.'

Keith does.

'Are you alright? Need anythin?'

'Nah, it's orright.'

I hear Dad rifling through some parts. Keith talks again.

'Might have to start thinkin lateral.'

'Whadda ya mean?'

'Dunno. It was on the telly the other night though. Bloke said ya gotta think lateral in the dairy industry. Try new stuff.'

'What, milk goats?'

'Dunno.'

Silence.

'Just look after yerself.'

'I'll be right.'

I hear one of them tearing a Stanley knife through a cardboard box.

'Tone it down at the pub, too, or you'll end up in the slammer, Doug Renfrey or not.'

'Gee, thanks, Dad.'

'Righto, smart arse, but just look after yourself.'

Silence.

'I'll be right.'

It starts raining, pretty heavy, and we're driving back down the main street. I'm already thinking of doing some reading on my bed, or listening to KISS records with my brothers if they'll let me, when Dad pulls the ute over, tells me to stay put, and runs into another shop called TAB.

Ten minutes later he walks out, ducks into the milkbar next door, and runs back to the car with his coat up over his head. He slams the door shut and hands me a Snickers. He smells like smoke.

'Don't tell Mum I went in there.'

I look at his crinkled face. 'Into the milkbar?'

'No, you wombat, the TAB! She'll start carryin on about your grandpa and there'll be no bloody let-up for weeks.'

'What about Grandpa?'

'That's enough, mate, no more alright?' Dad's voice is up a notch. 'Don't tell her anythin about the TAB, alright?'

'Okay.'

By the time we get home it's stopped raining, so Brian, Mick and I slip around and kick the footy on the front grass. Dad doesn't kick with us like usual. He sits in the ute in the garage and then, after about an hour, he slides it along the muddy track and back into town.

'Where did you go with Dad today, Stevie?'

I tell her all the places except the TAB.

In her apron, she looks at me, holding onto a wooden spoon covered in sloppy cake mix.

'You didn't go to the pub?'

'Nup.'

She goes back to grinding her cake mixture.

Dad's back just before dinner and bowls into the lounge room carrying a six-pack and a huge box of chocolates. Mum looks hard at his grinning face.

'You've been puntin.'

Dad looks at me like my hair's on fire.

'You bloody told her!' He moves in my direction.

'Lay off! He didn't say a bloody word. It's obvious . . .'

Dad looks down at me as I sidle toward Mum.

'After all I've told you, you go out puntin . . .'

Dad puts the chocolates and stubbies on the coffee table in the middle of the lounge. Out of both pockets he pulls cash tied together with lacker bands and slaps it down.

'I'll be able to keep the wolves from the door with that – and give a few of em a smack on the nose at the same time!'

Mum looks at the money then walks back to the kitchen.

'Course Stevie's got to come with me again. He's my lucky charm!'

If I was a real lucky charm that might have been alright. I could have been a little stone or badge buried in Dad's pocket. That way I could have been spared walking around racetracks everywhere from Leongatha to Sale and Melbourne to Penshurst.

For months, every Saturday morning, Mum would stand at the front door, yelling at him to leave me home. But he'd pack me up and off we'd go in the ute, him listening to race calls and blokes talking in numbers on the car radio. I'd be flicking through my fairytale books, Brothers Grimm or Hans Christian Anderson. And Dad didn't get stuck into me for reading them. He just tried to write tips on his form guide while he drove and smoked at the same time.

'How ya goin, lucky?'

Sometimes he'd say it reaching across and ruffling my hair, other times he'd have both hands on the wheel.

'Malright.'

'That's good, mate, that's good. Big day today.'

When we came up the track just before dark, Mum would be in one of the paddocks, rain, hail or shine. She'd stalk off in the opposite direction, our collie, Rastus, following behind her.

Every night, though, Dad would leave something different for her on the kitchen table: a bunch of flowers, some chocolates, or soft stuff wrapped in coloured tissue paper that he wouldn't tell me about. He'd stick some of the money down, wrapped in a lacker band, next to her present.

The first few times we went to the races the money was still there in the morning when we had breakfast. Mum would be silent and shaking her head, glaring at Dad or otherwise saying, 'Idiot', softly, and Dad would take the cash off the table before he cleaned up the dishes. But after we won big at the Geelong Cup – Dad said we were real lucky that day cos he put everything on the nose in the big one – the money was off the table by the time we got up.

After the Geelong Cup, Mum headed straight for the house whenever she saw us coming up the dirt track.

'How was yer day?'

Dad would slap the cash and present on the table, smiling. 'Not bad. How's yours?'

Without taking the rubber band off the folded pile, Mum would flick through the cash and smile. 'Not as good as yours.'

It was sort of my fault, I spose. I wasn't there and I was the lucky charm and I should have been there. But Mum said I'd miss school and she had to draw the line cos it was okay me going to the races and all of that on the weekend, but heading off on school days to the pokies across the border, no, she couldn't give the green light for that one.

Dad stood there and looked at Mum in the new pink slacks she wore around the house instead of tracky pants. After a while he smiled.

'Orright. I spose you're right.'

He went over and kissed her and then whipped off to pack his suitcase. He blew a kiss out the window of the ute while Mum stood on the porch and waved. I watched from behind the new velvet curtains.

He came back after us kids were all in bed on Thursday night, a day early. Mick and Brian didn't even bother to send me out. We could all hear well enough from our beds.

'How much did you lose!'

Silence.

'Answer me. How much?'

There was no answer. Mum yelled a bit more and Dad finally said a few things I couldn't make out cos he wasn't as loud as Mum. Then the house was quiet. We didn't even whisper to each other, but I heard Mick and Brian breathing little breaths and I knew they were awake like me.

I got up in the morning for school and Dad was asleep in the lounge-room chair, still wearing his jeans and yellow polo shirt.

Dad sleeps in the lounge chair. He goes to the toilet and sometimes outside onto the grass that's almost up to his knees and he stands there and stares. Then he's back into the chair to drink beer and watch TV and sleep.

Mum's in the paddocks most days, carrying her stick, walking in her gumboots with Rastus. Brian doesn't go to school – he goes milking with Mum. There are cows down the dirt track and one on the grass at the front of the house. The phone rings and Dad yells, 'Don't answer it!'

We eat stew out of cans and sometimes just vegemite and cheese on toast for dinner. Brian makes mine. Dad doesn't eat at all. He's put the rifle in its bag under the couch even though Mum's told him to put it away.

It's night and Dad's sitting in the chair – all the lights are off in the lounge, so I don't know if he's awake or asleep. Through the curtains Mum hasn't bothered to close, I see the lights of a car crawling toward the house, those lights getting rounder and bigger – yellow eyes creeping up the track.

'Mum, there's someone coming to visit.'

Dad stirs. Mum comes from some dark corner of the house and she's next to me, looking out the window.

'Who is it, Doug? *Who is it?*'

Dad doesn't say anything, but I think he's looking toward the open curtains and the lights coming toward the house and then turning off. Mum starts yelling.

'Boys get out! Get out! Out the back, into the paddock – *run*, don't stop, *run!*'

I dash to the kitchen but then stop, peer around the door. It's hard to see in the dark, but Mum's shape is bending toward Dad. In the funny shadows, it looks like she's got three legs, but then I realise one is her stick.

'Are you gunna do something?' she says.

Dad's head moves and then his shape steps out of the chair. He reaches under the couch and then Mum and Dad are six legs walking toward the front door.

Mick and Brian drag me through the back door and I'm running behind my brothers while they yell at me to keep up, across the bumps in the dark paddocks, puffing and thinking, Dad can do anything, he can, he can do anything.

Belief

I spose I thought I'd see more blokes with skullcaps on. Those little bloody caps without the peaks on the front. I don't know what I was thinkin. It's an old Jew hospital and all that, but course they're not gunna be wearin em down here in the kitchen, cleanin pots.

Shit no.

They're fucken huge pots. You can't get your arms into the bottom of the bastards. I dunno know how you're sposed to get em clean. I've been cleanin this one for I reckon three-quarters of an hour and there's still some brown shit down in it somewhere. I can feel it. Sort of spreads away, all soft and spewy when you touch it.

And you can hardly hear yourself think in here with all the clangin and steam comin out of sinks and water runnin into steel or other water. And blokes yellin and carryin on. Still it's better than workin in the Target warehouse. Too many young smart-arses bossin ya round. With their little beards and full of friggin attitude.

I was gettin enough boxes unpacked. Fuckheads.

Feel like the right-royal first-day dickhead in here though. Should ask the bloke at the sink next to me with the Yankees cap how ya sposed to get these things clean.

Nah, can't do that. But I wouldn't mind askin how many of em we're sposed to do. And when smoko is.

There's not many Jews here at all I don't reckon. The bloke behind me, he's workin at a sink, but he's got different pots to wash than me. Must have. He's laughin and havin a great time. Can't be a Jew either. He's got a bald head.

Weird bastards don't use the lights on Satdees. Can't figure that one out. And fucken Gutnick wouldn't go to the footy on Satdees even when he was the prezzy of Melbourne.

It's gravy on the sides of this bloody thing, I reckon. Feels like your mum's roast chicken gravy all over it and slippery. But Christ knows what's on the bottom of the thing though. Still I'm gunna have to get the fucker spick and span cos the rabbit or the rabbi or whatever down the end of the kitchen's gunna check it, like he's lookin at a centrefold, when I've finished with the bastard.

Yankees-cap told me before the silly cunt's makin sure the meat pots and the milk pots don't get mixed up. And that they're totally fucken clean. Don't know why. And parrently the reason why he keeps walkin up and down behind us is to make sure we don't accidentally flick anythin from our side of the kitchen onto the other side. The cunt's mad.

He gets right up close behind all the cleaners. Here he comes, look at him ... gets his big long black beard so it's almost down the guts of the pots. Look at that ... he grabs hold of the pots and pans and other shit with them see-through plastic gloves of his. And doesn't say anythin.

There's not much room between the meat-pot cleaners on this side and the milk-pot cleaners on the other side, so he squeezes through, not even sayin scuse me or anythin. Bumps into us, no sorrys, no nothin at all.

So I ask Yankees-cap why the rabbit doesn't say scuse me or sorry or anythin. Yankees turns to me, then looks at the rabbi a few metres away in his long black coat thing and hat that's too big.

'Cos we're gendile scum,' he says.

Buggered if I know what that means. But it doesn't sound good. I ask Yankees what a gendile is, but he doesn't hear me above the fresh water he's runnin into his sink.

The pots bang and ting and the blokes behind us, who I reckon are cleanin three pots to every one of mine, they chuck their clean ones along the bench for the old rabbi. I dig me hands right into the bloody pot and realise I'd better shift me arse or I'm gunna be here all day on this one. I reckon Yankees has knocked off three more than me.

I reach in tryin to find the bottom of the bloody thing when I feel stingin on me right hand. It's a real bastard. I scream, 'Fuck', really loud. It feels like I've cut me bloody hand.

Pot cleaners look round and see me pull me pink glove out of the suds. Then they go back to their scrubbin cos they already know what's the matter: there's a hole in me glove, lettin in close to boilin water.

Me hand's still stingin and I take the glove off and look at the red mark on me finger. Bugger it hurts. I run some cold water onto me finger but not for too long cos I can't afford to get too much further behind with me pots.

I ask Yankees where I can get a new glove. He says I better get a whole new pair cos I've got no hope of findin one to match the one that's still alright.

'All the sizes are fucked up,' he says.

So I chuck the fucked one in the bin and Yankees points down the end of the kitchen to a row of cupboards. They're down near where the rabbi's checkin a heap of pots. I pass him on me way, the silly bastard, with his head stuck down one of em.

Why don't they just have some pots for milk and some for meat, if it means that much to em? Probly cost em too much to label the bastards. I spose they'd need somethin from Pine Gap to do em with if they wanted labels that wouldn't fry in that friggin water.

I start goin through one of the cupboards lookin for gloves. There's pots without handles and broken shit everywhere. Nothin in there in the way of gloves though. I open another one and there's cans of beans and shit like that. So I go to another steel cupboard and I'm just about to open the door of the thing when the rabbi comes up next to me.

He stands there in front of the cupboard so I can't get into it. He looks straight at me. Says somethin I can't understand. He's got really dark eyes and he's not smilin at me. Looks mean.

'I'm lookin for gloves.'

I show him my right hand and then point to the good glove I'm still wearin, still covered in spewy brown shit.

He just keeps lookin back at me. Like I'm stupid. Then he says somethin else. I look at the bastard and grit me teeth.

'*Gloves*, mate.'

I hear someone behind me, above the clatter, sayin the rabbi speaks yiddish or somethin. I call back over me shoulder, at whoever it was, 'I don't care if he speaks bloody mandarine, I just want some gloves.'

Any kind'll do. I think the bloke behind me says somethin else, but I can't hear it above a big gush of steam.

I start gettin pissed off. I haven't even finished one fucken pot and the shift's been goin Christ knows how long and I don't really fancy headin back down to Centrelink again next week lookin for a job. And there's a friggin priest standin in front of me mumblin and I can't get any fucken gloves.

So I try to push past him, but he blocks me. Nice and solid. I try another direction but he's there. Too quick for me. I try back the other way, try goin under his arm but he grabs me in a headlock.

I go to punch him hard in the ribs. But he grabs the punch with his other hand and he's got me knackered. I give an almighty wriggle and manage to get free of him, but he kind of deflects me and I end up on the ground.

Strong bastard.

I'm on the tiles grabbin at his legs with one hand and tryin with me other one to open up the cupboard from the bottom. I'm pullin that hard on him that he almost loses his balance and I think I've got him.

But the bastard steps on me arm. Holds it down nice and tight. And it bloody hurts. I scream out. 'Shit. *Shit!*'

By this time there's three pot cleaners and two other Jews round us. The Jews are screamin at me in their yiddish and the pot cleaners are sayin, I think it's to me, 'That's the milk cupboard, *mate*, not the glove cupboard', and the rabbi's picked me up by the shoulders and pinned me against the cupboard. His nose is just about in me face.

The other Jews have quietened down a bit, enough so that a pot cleaner can talk to one of em. Thank Christ this Jew seems to know a bit of English. I can see him as I look over the rabbi's shoulder and his big hat's noddin along with his beard. Then he heads off somewhere else in the kitchen.

The pot cleaners tell the rabbi that it's alright, he can let me go. But he can't understand a thing they're saying so he just keeps me stuck up against the cupboard. I keep wrigglin to try to get free, but he's got me tied up, that's for sure. I say, 'Let me go, ya dickhead', and he just keeps on starin.

Then the other Jew comes back and he's got a long pair of pink rubber gloves in his hands. The rabbi lets me go, grabs the gloves off his mate and then locks me up again under the arms and hauls me back to me sink. He gives me the gloves, smiles even, then goes back to his pots.

I'm shakin a bit but I go back to mine too. I keep me head down and me gloves on.

The Favourite

Before I see his face, I see his penis. In a cage behind rusted bars he's sitting on his haunches. Then he looks at me – or rather I lift my head and look at him. Though I have never before seen his face, I know he is the boy from my dreams. Under the house, on my knees, I stare at him and then I hear my mother calling. Through a gap in the weatherboards I see her in the garden carrying the tomahawk she uses for splitting our firewood.

But the boy doesn't exist. And he never will. What I give you is the fantasy of a seven-year-old girl that has become an old woman's memory. This old woman is now an unreliable witness, even to herself. She is a woman who mumbles in front of her friends as if she were asleep. She is someone for whom a bed with hard sheets is waiting a few blocks away. It's a bed not far from an activities room where someone will play piano. She will sit among men and women her age, with rugs across their knees, and listen to melodies that seem to come from a radiogram never permanently turned off in her mind.

He doesn't exist but her mother is real.

She smiles and asks me to help in the kitchen, to take the knives to the drawer and place them inside, quietly, because she doesn't like the clatter and racket. I may lick the cake spoon – if I must – but not the inside of the bowl because that is a filthy habit, reserved only for those without manners and with no likelihood whatsoever of gaining any.

My mother wears a floral apron, walks from bench to table, flour covering her arms; flour joined with water and the sun through a kitchen window so that her arms begin to flake. My mother's whole body turns white, flakes and collapses to the floor as I lick the spoon. I see her in pieces on the wood floor and then her face is in front of me, speaking.

'Why are you looking at me like that?'

'Sorry, Mother.'

'You should be, young lady.'

Only women visit our property and they talk with my mother in the sitting room. From where I sit in the library I hear muffled voices. One afternoon I enter to ask for a glass of water and my mother and another woman together on a settee move suddenly away from each other. Then the stranger goes back to signing papers on the mahogany table and my mother shouts me out of the room.

I meet him in a dream.

I am underwater and the women around me wear iron suits and large yellow helmets with tubes extending from them and up toward the ocean's surface. I am as naked as when I get out of the copper tub at night, shaking droplets from my skin as my mother smiles and towels me. But she is not among the women underwater, the women whose mouths beneath their grills are saying that I must swim upward, quickly, because I have no breathing apparatus, I am drowning. Behind them a large fish swims and then appears too suddenly before my face, eyes dark and bulbous. In that moment he swims past, too, yet I don't see his face. But I see his nakedness, the roundness of his buttocks, his calves scissor-kicking, the length of his arms stretching and bending.

He is older than me.

In a lace nightgown, I lift myself onto my elbows and breathe salty, midnight air on this our inland farm. The curtains beside the open window are motionless and there is a crescent moon and the sound of a dog somewhere, far away, barking.

The dog stops barking and it is my birthday. I am ten years old and my mother turns to me at the breakfast table and explains that I will not be going to school until I am thirteen, if I am even to go to school at that age. There is, for certain, no need for me to go to primary school. My mother says there has never been a need for anyone to go to primary school because teachers with their bad breath and canes are snide and she should know, she says, she should know. My mother watches the willow tree branches trying to push through a kitchen window and I nod at her, but she doesn't see. I go to my room and gather my hat and gloves because it is the day for our weekly two-hour shopping trip to town and I must be ready when Mr Forsyth arrives with the horse and cart for our silent journey.

I sit between Mr Forsyth and my mother and watch his large and gnarled hands grip the reins, but I make sure my mother doesn't see me looking. When we get to town, men and boys are everywhere and my eyes widen until my mother stares down at me and prods me in the ribs with her index finger. I look at the ground, the footprints from large boots all up and down the red and orange dirt.

Between shops I take the risk and look up again. Men are talking on street corners, chins pointy under black hats, moustaches moving with smiles and laughter. I look at the hardness of the men's cheekbones and jaws and wonder what winds they have withstood to become so sharpened. They tip their hats at my mother and she ignores them as we pass. I hear muffled words and sometimes guffaws disguised to sound like coughs.

The one time I ask my mother where my father is she screams and cries for several hours and I can hear her no matter where I hide in the house or on the property, even the last gum tree at the fence line where our property borders the McTavishs'. The next morning when she finds me she says my father died when I was a baby. You don't remember him, she says, though it was a dream about him that made me ask his whereabouts. But my mother says I must have been imagining things because I can't remember him. I hold her hand and walk inside.

My mother showed me photo albums when I was young, filled mainly with pictures of me, dressed in white lace or wool, bonnet tied under my chin. But on some pages there are four triangles set at the corners of a square, a square that should have held a photo, another building block for memory. But now I have only the memory of a photo's absence, keeping unsteady the memory of someone who doesn't exist. Who shouldn't exist. My mother quickly flicked past the pages with gaps and later, I'm sure, the gaps are filled with photos of me.

We're standing on a street corner and Mr Forsyth drives his cart toward us. As ever I have not seen my father among the men in town. But I have seen the boy. No longer naked, no longer underwater, he is in men's eyes, in gruff voices calling out the price of fish or meat from market stalls. Mr Forsyth climbs down from the cart and pats his horses. My mother holds my hand and the boy is there in the way she does it. There in the warm fold of her hand itself.

Do you like the way it looks? It's real. Touch it.

There are always cake spoons to lick because my mother bakes relentlessly. Orange sponges, poppy seed, two-tiered hummingbird, black forest and caramel fudges. There are hedgehogs with sultanas as well as breadcrumbs, carrot cakes and fruitcakes and banana walnut loaves. Pikelets become my favourite but I do not tell her because previously I told her marble cake was my favourite and she stopped baking it.

Surely there are too many cakes for the two of us. Leftover slices are fed to the chickens and the occasional quarter cake, always cream, is in the rubbish pile. But the pikelets in the meatsafe; I know my mother doesn't like them. I haven't eaten them all, have I? I ask about them and soon, I recall, there are no more.

From the stairs late in the evening, I watch my mother knitting large garments. Some she lays on the hallway chest, coats for the horses to wear on winter nights. One night she carries to the door a smaller garment, freshly knitted, opens the door and returns without it.

I enter school and despite the gaps in my memory and education I also enter university because my mother assures me it is essential for a woman to have an exemplary education. At university I read Sigmund Freud and I think I understand that my life is partly an imagining. The boy has been a waking dream, a phantasm – the creation of an unconscious at war with a mother and indebted to a dead or missing father.

The lecturer stands tweed-suited at the front of the auditorium and continues the therapy that began when I was a young girl and the psychiatrist entered my room, the night the police brought me back from roaming in the night. The lectures concluded after several years and my mother died soon after they finished and then more therapy followed for me. Free association lying on a leather couch, afternoons of Rorschach drawings that seem now also to be dreams. Lectures, dreams or sessions, they all fill me now with the wish that I could believe everything I am telling is but a symbol, dragged from my unconscious because no one could possibly remember what I believe has happened.

It is in the asylum – how long ago? – that I first cry out. 'He's real. Oh my Lord, he's real.'

The exclamation is one among many, of mine and others'; a cry born from too much or not enough medication, bouncing off the white walls of the mid-twentieth century, raised from convulsive therapy or panic, the nurses come to inject with soft dreams.

Don't tell her that you know. She'll kill me. You're imagining me ... Can you do that?

I see him in dreams in the weeks before I meet him. Or are they dreams I had after I met him and he left my life? Or my life left me.

I am flying above clouds in a plane that doesn't have an outer casing, yet navy-uniformed and smiling hostesses I've seen in my mother's magazines parade the aisles, their hair-dos tightly bunned and secure under hats glued to their heads, their skirts not so much as rippling in the wind.

He is a voice speaking from where the cockpit of the plane should be. Then he is a cloud and then a pig in a pen that turns to his human shape, a muscled back, buttocks tight on his frame, but no face.

In the dream the plane never lands and the boy under the house is five years, I guess, maybe six years, older than me.

My mother is coming with an iron axe. With teeth that burr with machinery.

Twenty-five, is it thirty years ago, I am reading Freud, or possibly Jung, in my cell over and over and the doctors walk past, no longer bothering to open the door and ask what I'm reading. I have discovered another universe and I slip my hands into it through the pages and pull them out covered in stars.

My mother hands me another spoon and I lick it.

My mother gives me a puppy. I lose it one afternoon while she bakes. I look up at her smiling face in the kitchen window. I search, below the window, push past the pittosporums and agapanthus that seem to be more and more flowers but then become a mural painted on the weatherboards. The mural has a door with an open padlock and later at university I read about the significance that locks possess in dreams.

I crouch down and enter the door, climb under the house, to the smell of rotting vegetables and cakes and I see a shape in a cage – a pig? – and I am not dreaming or speaking, I am not, and the pig makes no sound. He is there. Not in the eyes of any man in town or the memory of my father who I have never met. He is there.

Put your hand there . . . that's it, yes. Now rub . . .

The freight train stops at the station and the boy climbs on. In the darkness I make out the shape of his hand reaching for mine. I hold my hand out and though I can feel my body pushing my hand toward holding his, I don't grip it.

I watch him in the carriage doorway, the train edging slowly down the track, his face visible for a moment under yellow light then gone. I wander away, aimlessly into the night, until I am picked up by the police and taken to Mother, who smiles to have me back and holds me. At least this would be how things were if I had not read in university about what the unconscious is trying to say when it imagines trains and what it means to be taken home to Mother rather than catching a train with my brother, who has escaped from my mother and from me and yet has taken me or my imaginings with him. Yet there is a something of me that remains in the company of my mother.

The day after I meet him I still see his penis and his face and my mother's tomahawk and I am in the kitchen with her and she's baking a cinnamon bun, then it's on the table, wafting sugar heaven into the sunlight.

'Mother, do I have a brother?'

Her face turns to icing. White and candleless. Then she laughs and flushes.

'What kind of a thing to say?'

I look at the fullness of her breasts, the round smile of her cheeks.

'I just wondered.'

I run to my room.

That feels good, just there. Now harder ... Use your mouth now.

The police bring me back and the same night or the next night the psychiatrist is in my room, bowler hat and glasses. My mother says I cannot go downstairs, I must be in my bed where I can be monitored. The psychiatrist helps me with my imagination. Investigates it. Asks it questions. Tells me imagination is an interesting thing, but we cannot trust it. It must be trained, broken, like we train and break a horse, like my horse, Merrick.

'Do you remember when you first rode him? Did he buck? Yes? Your imagination is difficult to ride. But it can be broken.'

He goes with me into my imagination, then goes with me beneath the house. Or is under the house now in my room? There are empty cans and broken porcelain plates in the earth. Turned earth. Freshly turned, I'm sure. No mural. Pittosporums and agapanthus undisturbed in front of the weatherboards. Then we're standing beneath my mother's kitchen window and I can see her, hands in the sink, and I can smell pikelets in the oven.

I am a witness to what is real. And what is imagination. And whatever exists between the two. A witness also to whatever a therapist believes or a mother denies or the dream about a brother foretells. I am an old woman ready to be taken this afternoon to where there are hard sheets and harder nurses. All their eyes are black, they will be, and I hear now a knocking on the door and then a key that opens it. My daughter enters, hair in a bun, the way my mother wore her hair when baking.

I am an old woman and I am unlocking him again and he is leaving his cage. I cry and tell him I am sorry, that I could have unlocked him sooner if I had not enjoyed the playing. He is an old man smiling and saying they were better than the games our mother had played. Then he is a young boy and crying and running through wild flowers and a paddock in the night, past the gum trees, sentinels that line the fence and gate, and I am running with him. I watch him running ahead of me, wearing my long pants; he is an 'itinerant worker', that is our ruse if we are questioned.

My mother isn't coming into this or any room to take me to hard sheets. She carries a cake spoon, she has lost her tomahawk and doesn't know where to find it. The policeman knocks on the door and she bends down and holds me and whispers, doesn't she, that they will never know and you will never know, either. And then she looks at me and hugs me again and says aloud, 'My lovely, beautiful boy.' The policeman doesn't hear the slip. He walks away and my mother scowls.

I lower my head to the pillowcase of my new bed and the lights go out and on again and photo albums fly in front of me, their pages turning. I see photographs of men in town, waiting on street corners, then one man, then a boy; photos float to the ground while the light flickers on and off; a boy, a man, an elderly man, asleep, hands folded and shut into a kitchen cupboard while my mother bakes.

What is your favourite, darling, what is it? I will make it for you.

Story Board

In her red Honda Integra, Cait drove past rows of weather-board homes and nature strips dotted with trees too small to offer privacy to the houses. But she felt distant from her elusive subject, so she started getting out of the car and pacing the footpaths. She talked to elderly women braving the beginnings of winter and doing their gardening. After-ward, she sat in her car and scribbled notes about the women's speech patterns. Illuminating character studies, but Cait felt the need to go deeper, to push herself.

She had to. There was so much expectation on her after her hit debut film, *The Memory War*.

Breathe in the atmosphere, that's what she had to do, immerse herself in this outer western suburb. Up until two weeks ago she hadn't known Eccles Park existed, with its broken swings in playgrounds, graffitied paling fences and basketball courts with smashed backboards. She felt a twitter in her stomach as she padded footpaths in black clothes after midnight, prowling in the sickly yellow light, a glow caused by smog, she thought, but wasn't sure. She peered at dark front yards and the closed venetian blinds, the smell of some kind of industry floating through the powerlines, so strong she sometimes pressed her fingers over her nostrils.

She wasn't sure what it was she was searching for. But that was always the fun part of a project; the delicious uncertainty about whether the desire inside her to tell a story would actually match up with something out there in the real world. Stories had to come from somewhere. They bubbled up out of what people called the unconscious but Cait called the 'pre-known'. Once the story overtook her, she always found out what she already knew. There was a kind of certainty about the pre-known.

God, could she ramble on! Yet this was the kind of philosophical banter that funding bodies and journalists liked to hear. But for Cait, at night in Eccles Park, it was just the excitement, the tingle in her stomach, that kept her looking for what she already knew she would find.

On a pale night when her breath smoked white in front of her, Cait walked past another weatherboard house, this one double-storey with a double carport. Maybe it was the boxing kangaroo with what looked like a drawn-on Karl Marx moustache in one of its front windows, or the birdbath in the yard, but there was something iconic about this house. Bigger than those around it, it seemed to have bossed itself, a squat giant seagull on a night beach, into its position between the grey paling fences.

Cait walked up and down in front of it, stopped under trees further down the street, looked at the house's dark outlines from different angles. She walked past it on the footpath opposite and as she did she heard a door slide open and the slow clop of footsteps under the double carport. She hid in a large clump of bushes across the road.

Cait saw the glowing red end of a cigarette appear, attached to the darkness of a human shape that she would later learn was Craig Stone. He leant against what she thought was a Toyota Hilux and the red glow brightened then dulled.

She looked at her watch: 2.33. This guy should be in bed. Why's he up? Is his wife awake? His kids? What's he thinking?

Good, she thought. I'm asking all the right questions.

On her haunches, Cait shivered, folded her arms and smiled.

Who *is* this man, smoking and, most likely, staring into the yellow sky? What has driven him from his bed?

Cait watched the Craig shape lower the red glow to his side, then raise it again to his head. She tried to hold back her shivers and she whispered to herself, 'This is the one.' Her eyes fixed on the cigarette glow, she ran her hands over her tights. She felt a run in her right leg and knew she must have got it jumping into the bushes. But she smiled and thought, You don't get to know what happens in suburban Australia by sleeping safe in freshly washed sheets. You have to be up, peering into the night. Finding out where the night lives and what it plans to do.

Normally, in any other suburb, Cait would march to a stranger's front door and ring the bell. But the next day in front of the Stones' house, she stood on the footpath, as observant as she'd been the night before. She looked at the 'Young and Free' sticker on the back of the Hilux and thought, I'm in deep.

This wasn't suburbia, it was unurbia. A dark Commodore purred past and a bald-headed man with wraparound shades and a sharp beard turned to look at her. She watched the Commodore shrink around the bend, then turned back and looked at the house. Perhaps she could try another. Or another suburb.

Her thoughts ricocheting, Cait bounced on her heels, said, 'Stuff it', and felt her legs carry her up the Stones' driveway, past the birdbath and onto their front porch.

'Yeah, wotcha want?'

It wasn't Craig who opened the door, but a woman; a woman with one brown tooth on her top row and some hastily applied pink lipstick. Her large, unfashionable sunglasses appeared locked into position on her forehead. She smelt of uncooked sausages.

'Ahh, I'm from the ...'

A man's voice came from somewhere inside the house.

'If it's that bloody Optus, tell em to clear out ...'

Cait smiled. 'I'm not from Optus ... I'm from the telly ...'

The owner of the voice appeared in the hallway and stood behind his wife. His wavy black hair trailed over his ears and he wore a white Lee t-shirt over his muscular chest.

'How are ya?' he smiled.

His voice, despite the ocker twang, was like chocolate

melting just before you swallowed it. Cait glanced at his tanned arms, her favourite part of a man.

'Good thanks,' she said, noticing that his jeans, now side-by-side with his wife's fat thighs in black hotpants, were filled with footballer's legs.

The woman looked at her husband, scowling. Then she hawked her frizz of bottle-blonde hair in Cait's direction.

'What show?'

'Pardon?' Cait said, grinning and looking now at the man's moustached smile.

'You said you were from the telly . . .' the woman spat, standing closer to her husband.

'Yes, that's right,' Cait said, trying to look directly at the woman.

'You come bout the kids?' the woman quizzed, her head bending upward.

Kids? Great, whatever.

'Yep, I'm here about the kids . . . And you two as well . . .'

The woman half smiled.

It always worked. In the suburbs, if you're from the telly you're from real life. You're someone. Cait didn't talk about her arthouse movies until much later.

'Want a cuppa?' the man said, straightening his smile as his wife speared a look at him.

Cait said she did and followed the back muscles in the man's t-shirt down the corridor to the kitchen, silently chastising herself for not observing more of the house.

Sitting at her computer after her first meetings with the Stones, Cait tried to concentrate and express, succinctly, her sense of the forming story: 'When true love lies.' Yeah, she liked that, a double entendre. It was a bit close to *Where the Truth Lies* with Kevin Bacon, and even, she supposed, Schwarzenegger and Jamie Lee Curtis's *True Lies*. But that movie was years ago, American, and not at all suburban, not at all her story. Anyway, she thought the next day, scratching in her notebook in the Stones' front yard while watching Craig tie up his boots on the front step, 'when true love lies' wasn't going to be the title. And why was she thinking about titles? No point getting to the final page when she hadn't even started a draft.

Craig left the steps and walked under the carport. Cait grinned at the years between his black stubby shorts and fashion. But she watched the hairs on the backs of his thighs disappear past the Hilux and into the backyard. The Stones' kelpie barked, Craig told it to shut up and Cait heard the aluminium shed door close.

She didn't know yet if she'd use it – it had the potential for cliché so she'd have to be careful – but Craig was a recovering alcoholic. Beer bottles leaning against the wheelie bin would have been a great motif, but also a bit hackneyed. If she added an empty whisky bottle or two, just leant them against the bin ...

It could work.

A year ago Jill told Craig it was either her or the grog. He wouldn't tell Cait why, but after the ultimatum he chose Jill straight away. Despite Craig's mysteriousness, it was all too neat. She knew she'd have to elongate Craig's decision-making process. Add some violence because, Jill told her, Craig was a *lazy* drunk, not a *punchy* one. Anyway, the important thing was that Craig chose Jill, not the grog. He wouldn't be there if he hadn't, and that would have meant no glowing cigarette under the carport and no Cait in Craig's backyard, up close and smelling his aftershave that, she had to admit, was not the Brut 33 she'd expected.

Cait sips the strong tea Craig's made for her then lowers the cup to her waist. Craig puts a saw up on a contraption, the name of which Cait knows but has forgotten. She watches him steady the wood on it and she thinks again of how much he looks like Michael Caton. Her friend Louise at Warner knew Caton well, often went to dinner at his house, and given the success of *The Memory War*, Louise would probably put in a call for her.

'So, this research, it's for *Current Affair* or somethin?'

That drawl of his makes her skin tingle. She shakes her head and doesn't know if she's doing it for Craig or to clear the fuzz in her head.

'It's background reporting for *Four Corners*.'

'My gunna be famous?'

Craig smiles and Cait smiles back. She holds his eyes too long, wondering if he's holding hers.

'I said you won't be on camera, remember? You're not going to ask me about this again, are you Craig?' She smiles, meets his eyes again and then looks away to the neighbour's Hills Hoist peeking over the fence.

'Sorry, bit slow,' he grins.

A cigarette in his mouth – sometimes he's *too* perfect – Craig turns on his buzz saw. He lets it scream through a few old fence palings. The mug is warm in her hands and she can smell something porky chocolate in the air that Craig has told her is the abattoir a couple of kilometres north. The saw stops screaming.

'Why aren't you at work today?' she asks.

Craig pulls his cigarette from his mouth. He holds it in front of his chest and grins at her.

'Do I have to tell you again, Cait?'

She holds her mug down low and lets her lips flicker slowly into another smile. She bends her head sideways at him and she's sure he gets a quick look at her breasts.

'I work swingshift at the glass plant. Some mornings, some arvos, nights. Never know where I am ... Neither does anyone around here,' he laughs, looking away to the kitchen window. Cait follows his gaze to where Jill is framed, her head bent over the dishes.

The saw roars and bits of fence fall flat on the grass. The kelpie noses around the lawn and barks at the saw until it stops. Craig tells it to sit down.

'Tell me more about what happened with Jill.'

He butts his cigarette on the grass with a quick twist of his faded black boot. One hand back on the saw, he shows Cait the open palm of his other hand. He lowers an eyebrow and his smile's gone.

'Ask her.'

The saw screams.

Cait didn't like talking to Jill. First, there was her face, that tooth and her menopause rose-flush. And then there was her accent and grammar.

'When the kids first come from the orpho, I give em a whole bunch of toys, ya know, cos they dinnin have no real good stuff back there wiff em.'

That would have to be adjusted for her characterisation. People might talk like that in real life, but it just went too far into that Aussie under-culture stuff and Cait didn't want her film slipping into that territory. Jill also wore clanging gold bracelets, some of them genuine, and she stared at Cait but never into her eyes. But like it or not, Jill, or the character she would become, was the squelching heart of the story.

'He stopped wiff the grog but it come too late. He was knackered.'

Cait asked her to explain.

'Shootin blanks.'

Cait moved the digital recorder closer to Jill on the kitchen table. Through the window they could both see the washing flapping and spinning on the line: white sheets, blue and white singlets and assorted men's underwear; hipsters in green and red. Jill kept looking over at the washing and the grey sky, saying she might have to 'get that all off there'. Cait smiled at the hipsters, found herself imagining them on Craig and then wished she had a mug to hold. But Jill had never offered her anything to drink.

'So you started doing foster care ...'

'Always wantedta.'

'How many kids have you fostered in, say, the last five years?'

'Dunno. Gotta be thirty or more ... Hang on, nah, sprobly closer to fifty.'

Two of the fifty came running into the kitchen and Cait paused the recorder. Jill wiped both the kids' noses and sent them on their way, followed by nappy smell.

Craig had told Cait he would have preferred the lounge to himself to watch the football and the Grand Prix, but she asked anyway.

Jill laughed.

'He wanted to get back on the booze after the first couple turned up. Ease orright now.'

'Why was Craig a drinker in the first place, do you think, Jill?'

She screwed up her nose.

'Cos he's a bloody drongo's why.'

Cait smiled and Jill added, 'But ease orright now.'

Craig walked past the window holding a huge black garbage bag to his chest, his muscles tight in a blue cut-off shirt. He nodded at Cait. She smiled back at him then looked at Jill. Her eyes were narrow.

'Looks afta the joint,' she said, loud and staring straight at Cait.

One of the kids ran into the kitchen again and jumped onto Jill's lap.

'How much do you get paid to support each child?'

Jill stood up.

'It's spittin. Gotta get all that off ...'

It takes a couple of weeks, but Cait reaches the inner sanctum. Craig's shed.

On the workbench, shiny saw blades and jars full of nails, screws and washers. The walls hold rusty blades hanging from even rustier nails. She half expects to see that poster of a girl playing tennis, her back to the camera, putting a ball into her short skirt, hitching it up to reveal a smooth and underwear-free bum. Cait looks at her own skirt. Her best black one, thin green tights underneath. Watching Craig screw something onto the engine he's pulled free from the lawn mower, she smooths her skirt and steps closer to him where he stands behind his workbench.

'You do everything yourself?' she asks.

He looks up and smiles.

'You see anyone else round here for the job?'

He's stopped working and his eyes roll over her.

'No,' she says, looking away at the hammers on hooks, 'only you Craig.' Yes, some of those hammers would have to be replaced by a calendar. With an impossibly tanned woman in a white bikini. Cait looks back at Craig and his eyes are still on her. She holds his gaze, feels breath slide up from her lungs.

'You live far from here?' he says to the inner workings of the engine.

She doesn't even need to do this interview. The story

is structured and settled. It's stored in a computer, backed up on disk, the first treatment already in the hands of her agent, twenty-five kilometres from here in the middle of the CBD: the beaten wife of an alcoholic husband fosters more kids than an NGO and wins her husband's heart through the power of her self-sacrificing love. The AFI will fund it, Cait will, of course, direct it, co-write the script and, she thinks, it will at least make back the five or so million invested.

'I live a long way from here, Craig,' she says, sipping the Coke he's given her and standing so close to him now she can see the mole on his right ear lobe. Craig takes a rag to the engine and dabs it.

'Same city though, hey?' he says, his head still bent over the engine.

He looks up and she smiles down at the stained concrete floor. When she looks up again, she says, 'Yeah, same city.' But Craig has pulled the ripcord on the detached engine and it's roaring.

He looks at her, grinning, and mouths, 'What?'

She yells, 'Same city!' as he turns off the engine and Cait watches its tiny wheels do a final spin before the motor coughs and stops.

Craig is out from behind the workbench, stepping toward her. Cait stiffens and turns to look at the open shed door.

The Hero

I'd never been one to get up in the night for a piss. I could usually hold on till morning, no matter how many beers I'd had the night before.

The old man could never hold on. But he wouldn't go out to the shithouse. Too cold for him he reckoned, even in summer. So he'd get out of bed and stand up and piss into an ice-cream container. Then he'd stick it back under the bed. I remember Mum emptying it into the shithouse in the morning before I went to school.

I could always hang on. But then I turn fifty and suddenly I'm getting up for a piss in the night.

When I first started I crept round tryin to make sure I didn't wake up Mum. Looks like there was no use worrying about that. She was probably lyin awake in her room anyway.

It must have been the last op that had me up and about. When they dug around in me guts they must have buggered up the waterworks somehow. It wasn't like I was gettin on the grog more. Christ, they'd been in and out of me guts that many times it's a wonder piss didn't fall through holes and into me muscles. What's left of em.

I'd go out of me bedroom, make a left-hand turn and

head off along the corridor. I'd keep me head down so I didn't whack into that bloody stupid cuckoo clock thing hangin on the passage wall for Christ knows what reason. It ticks, but the bird never comes out of it.

Then I'd walk through the kitchen in me bare feet, cross the cold lino and head out to the dunny in the lean-to, with a door you can't pull shut cos there's lino sticking up and I'm buggered if I could ever fix it.

I bumbled round in the dark. Me eyes are ratshit and the doc reckoned it was the smokes that did that. He said, 'Pete, how can you smoke so much when your father died of emphysema?' I said somethin like, 'It's pretty bloody easy, mate: you grab one out of the pack, like this, and then ya ...'

The doc shook his head and wrote a script out for me.

The old boy carked it a few years back. While I could still drive I'd get Mum in the car every week – every day for a while – and we'd head up to the cemetery. She'd stick petunias on his plaque and I'd watch her and wonder how much those blokes at the front gates were makin, doubling up and sellin flowers they nicked off the graves.

Mum always came out with the same bullshit while we were there.

'Your father was a hero ... There were a lot of fellows who didn't go, you know. And he went when he was sixteen ...'

I was born after he got back from the war. All I

remember was a pisspot bastard who gave me a beltin till I left home not long after the age he went off to fight.

We'd walk back to the car and she'd crap on about songs, parades and the empty town when the boys were away. I'd be thinkin, Christ, how does a bloke go from beltin his wife and kids to bein a hero? He was a bloke who did the normal tour of duty but you'd reckon he'd won the Vic Cross. When Mum pulls out the little black jewel case every Anzac Day I don't see much more than a service medal in there.

Saw a shrink once. *Once*. He reckoned I was at war with the old man. Said it was why I liked a drink – is that a *crime*? – why me marriages busted up and why I used to go walkabout a bit. He'd probly say it's why I need all the pills the doc's had me on for years. Just cos I wash me hands a fair bit and take a while gettin me daks on.

I used to get in a cuppla blues at the pub. That's not a war though, that's havin a stoush.

Got a job now – technically speaking. They said I could come back when I got better. Part-time washin windows in one of those get-off-your-arse-and-back-to-work set ups. But after the last op, I ended up in bed a fair bit and didn't manage to get back on the job. Plus I was in and out of hossy there for a while. Nurses are pretty nice when you've had your guts looked at. Sweeties. Lot bloody nicer than the ones in the cuckoo ward.

I used to like me job. But it's good in one way that

I've been home all the last year or so. Mum's gettin on — she's eighty-somethin. I can keep an eye on how she is — and it's not real good. But she still cooks a bewdy of a roast. Not that I've been able to eat much at all lately. Nothin really.

When I started getting up for a piss the house was real quiet. I could only hear the clock ticking and the fridge buzzing when I went through the kitchen. Then one night I got up and I could hear it: *music*. Comin from Mum's room, old country and western stuff. She never played music during the day at all. Most that was ever on was the telly from about six at night, and before that I had the tranny on with the races. No music.

But it was country and western twang comin out of her room in the middle of the night. I stood at me door for a minute or so then crept down the corridor for a piss and came back. She must have heard me up and about cos when I got back the music was off.

I remembered that music from somewhere. It took a while but then I remembered where from. Mum used to play it for the old boy when he was dying. Didn't think she liked it herself.

When I was with me first wife I came back a few times to visit him and Mum. Just to see what the old prick was up to. And that music would be on and I remember the name of the record: *Hymns of Gold*, some old country and western bloody church record.

'Just a closer walk with *theeee* . . .' with banjo and twang twang guitars.

Mum used to go to church way back when. The old boy never went, but he packed her and us kids off there every Sunday. Said it would do us some bloody good. He sat at home and sucked long necks with his mates.

Day after the music I sat with Mum at the table eatin tomato sandwiches. She had a couple. I could only get through half a one. Felt like me guts was gunna fall out the arse end of me.

I didn't tell her I'd heard the music. Thought, Shit, not my business, let her go. She's done it tough. Christ, the old boy gave her a hammerin. If it wasn't with his fists it was with his tongue. These days you'd get put in jail just for what he said to her.

When I came back to live with him and Mum after the trouble with me landlord, he gave me a tongue lashin, don't you worry. Said I was a pisspot and a bloody vagrant and no son of his was gunna be a vagrant and a fucken drunk. I told him that was the pot callin the kettle black and the old bugger, crook and suckin on an oxygen bottle, he still tried to take a swipe at me.

Mum hardly ever bit back. She put up with all his bull-shit, nursed him till he fell off the perch. He toned down a bit in the last year or so before he went, so now he's a saint in her eyes and that's that.

Still, if she wanted to forget all the other shit, that was fine by me. Her business. If she missed him and needed to play his songs at night, I thought, Well, that's up to her. Whatever she has to do.

But she started lookin crook round that time I reckon. Thinnin out. I wasn't eatin much either, but she was always up and about. Sometimes got me breakfast in bed cos I was a bit slow gettin goin in the morning. Didn't get up at all till lunch some days.

So she ran round and got more skinny and she wasn't as chirpy anymore. She looked like an old boot most days, hair everywhere, white dressing gown with a stain or two and bits of cotton hangin off it. I didn't get out of me PJs much, but she only ever got dressed, far as I could tell, when someone rang up and said they were comin over. Then the floral number was on, there'd be a pot of tea – *leaves*, not bags – and she'd have friggin scones on the table. I couldn't really eat one without chuckin it up but it would have been nice if a scone had turned up for me. Still, I usually headed off for a rest in bed not long after people came over. It buggered me out to chinwag too much.

Mum's not lookin any better these days. Her hair's gettin whiter.

Not long back, it took a big effort, but I got out of bed. She was sittin in the lounge knittin some bloody thing or other for a grandkid and the sun was through the window on her dressing gown and white hair and she looked like a fucken angel. Nearly brought up me pills when I saw her. She thought I was spewin up again so she turned round and picked herself up and said, 'Son, are you alright? What's going on? Are you alright?'

'Just a closer walk with *thee*, grant it Jesus if you *please* . . .'

When I was still gettin up for a piss, how many times did I hear that friggin song comin out of her room? After a month or two of the late-night entertainment, I said to her when we were eatin our boiled eggs at breakfast, 'Why you playin that music, Mum?' And she looked sideways toward the telly and the stereo.

'What music?'

'Not now, Mum. At night. I hear you playin your tape deck when I get up for a piss.'

I felt a bit embarrassed so I looked down at me placemat. Then I looked up and this time she was peering away toward the kitchen. I saw her chest rise up but I didn't hear her breathe in.

'I'm not playin any music, son. I'm dog-tired at night and sleeping. You must be dreaming.'

I looked at her and thought, Whatever you've gotta do, Mum.

I pulled myself up from the table and wandered out to the passage. I was about to head to me room when I remembered I needed the *Form Guide* if I was goin to get Mum to run up to the TAB and put a bet on for me. I came up to the living-room door again but then I pulled back and looked round the corner and hoped she wouldn't see me.

She had a picture frame in her hand and she was lookin at it and I couldn't tell, she might have been cryin. She wasn't makin any noise, she was just standin there and lookin at the picture. The old man was a prick of a bloke, but I spose if you've been with someone fifty-odd years you've gotta miss em when they go. Poor old chook, I thought, her heart's breakin up.

When she put the photo down and headed to the kitchen I nicked back in and grabbed the *Form Guide*. I looked at the photo she'd pulled out from the bunch on the buffet and I thought, Oh, shit, now her brain's breakin up as well.

It was a picture of me, all bright and shiny at me first wedding.

I'm never out of bed now. Mum said I should head into hospital, but with her lookin the way she is I'm not bloody goin anywhere. She's that crook she's even teary when she comes into me room. She's stuck a plastic ice-cream bucket under me bed and I pull it out and have a piss lyin down when I wake up at night.

The bedroom door's closed, but when I'm pissing I can hear, 'I am *weeaeek*, but thou art strong . . . Just a closer walk with *theeeee* . . .'

She must really be missing the old boy – the bloody music's really loud now. I lie awake and listen to it twangin away till I fall back to sleep.

A Redundancy

Max Richards is sitting across the table from me and stubbing out his cigarette. A slow grinding movement and it lies crumpled in a black plastic ashtray. From the top pocket of his suit he pulls out a packet, flips it open and taps the bottom of it. One cigarette rears up from the others. He pulls it out, then lays the packet on his palm in front of me.

I say, 'No thanks, I'm driving.'

Through the open doors of the coffee lounge I see a few eager suits making for work, strobed-up in the orange flash of street-sweeper lights. An almost empty tram hums past. Then everything's quiet again.

Max clicks once on a silver lighter and his cigarette comes to life behind a slow suck of air. He lets the smoke file through his nose and puts the packet on the green laminex table.

'The trouble with you journos,' Max says, 'is you don't really want to tell anybody about people like me. You think you do, but you don't.'

I look around the coffee lounge. It's empty except for a man with a black moustache in a royal-blue coat. He's moving around empty chairs and booths, polishing sugar dispensers and wiping down tables. The walls are covered in posters of Italian soccer teams from the eighties and I keep getting a waft of the toilet out the back.

What would I be doing in a shit-hole like this – *at this time of day* – if I wasn't interested in his story?

'Well, we'll see, won't we?' I say and take a bite out of my toast.

I pick up my mug and slurp on its contents, then look in Luigi's direction. Where does he get the gall to call this a cappuccino? I'm starting to sound like the wankers on the arts round, but I also know I haven't drunk coffee this bad since that trip to cover the by-election in Benalla.

I notice Max isn't drinking one. He could have warned me. But he's too busy getting all philosophical.

The suit boys at St Kilda Road gave me the story last week. Said old Maxey liked to talk in circles. Said, too, that if I *was* to look him up I should keep smart. And not smart arse.

Detective McEwan had leant back on his chair and puffed out that chest of his.

'You know what rock spiders are, Drew. Well, Max Richards is another kind of spider altogether, mate. And we can't pin a bloody thing on him. But I'll tell you what the cunt's up to . . .'

We haven't covered Max's type before, not since I've been at the *Age*, anyway. Not *newsy* enough. And there's a good chance this bastard won't be newsy enough either.

But, shit, I have to try something. If I don't get a few

by-lines soon I'll be drinking cappuccinos in Benalla again. And this time I'll be on their fucking local rag.

So here's old Maxey, sitting and munching on a mixed grill – looking relaxed and comfortable, thanks very much – and talking to me as he chews.

'It's you guys who made me redundant, you know!'

He laughs and cuts hard into his steak. A fried egg slides out of the way. His cigarette sits jealous and steaming in the ashtray.

'Well, at the very least you made me take a kind of different angle on things, didn't you?'

I'm looking at this Max Richards now. Solid bastard. But not fat. Long arms that look like he's stolen them from someone else. Hair's gone brown with an orange tinge – hit the bottle to stamp out the grey. Must be the mid-forties crisis thing. Can't wait till I get to that little milestone.

And he's decked out in the slick black suit with a matching tie like the businessman. Because, apparently, he is.

'So you run a couple of transport firms and a software company ...'

'Yeah, that's right. And I'll have you know, boy, the software packages have nothing to do with sex.'

He looks straight at me and grinds his molars on his steak. He keeps his eyes on me as he pulls a bit of gristle from his mouth and puts it on the side of his plate. I take another gulp of whatever's in my mug. He wraps the gristle in a serviette.

We eat and bullshit for a while about his businesses. I try to fit the Collins Street-type with what he used to do after hours as a younger bloke. And what I've heard he's up to now.

Time to get down to it.

'You said before that blokes like me are making you redundant. What's that all about?'

He stops eating. Puts his fork and knife at right angles on the plate and picks up the cigarette. He looks down at the tape recorder I've stuck between us and talks real slow.

'Look, you might by now realise I'm no fool.' The smoke's hanging around us like we're in a sauna and I almost want to cough. 'And I know you've heard at least a little bit about me, haven't you, or you wouldn't be here. So I won't keep you in suspenders.' He grins and drags on his cigarette. 'I couldn't keep beating poofs if you blokes were reminding everyone they're human, could I? If the man-in-the-street starts to think somebody's hard done by . . . well . . .'

I turn up the volume on the recorder.

'. . . everything's different then, *isn't it*?'

He lets the words hang in the air until they fall back toward the table and onto his food. He chops away at his eggs.

I look at him, wondering how much rope I need to throw him to hang himself with.

'What's different? You? The world . . .'

'I haven't worked it all out yet. I don't know where things fit.'

He looks around as if he means the coffee lounge, then butts out his cigarette and lights another one.

'It's hard to make things fit ... life's all bits and pieces, isn't it?' I say.

'It's just how things are. I don't know what I think of it. It just keeps happening. It's all a bit ...' He looks at me with his brown eyes and gets a bit of a smile going. 'I suppose it's like a job or a business. You've got to keep adapting. You know, *evolve*. Or something like that.'

He knocks away some of the cigarette. I change tack, start grilling him about his old life. Turns out he built up the transport businesses in the eighties during the day and gay-bashed at night. He was in his late twenties, early thirties. Him and his mates, drinking until the pubs closed in Mount Eliza. Poor little rich boys heading off in an RX7 to St Kilda Esplanade, looking for gays in public dunnies, kicking in the doors where they were having it off and beating the shit out of them. Leaving them lying in piss and whining on the floor.

'I must admit I loved to kick them in the balls. It's a bit bland looking back, I know, but I suppose I wanted to teach them what they were for. Not very creative ...'

He's looking at his grill and not chopping any of it and I look at him again. My coffee mug's empty. Thank Christ.

'Do you want another one?'

I shake my head.

'You think I'm an arsehole, don't you?'

I don't answer his question. I fold my hands in front of me and lean forward just a little bit across the table.

'Why did you start bashing them?'

He eyeballs me.

'People'd say I'm a homophobe, but as far as I can tell, that would mean I was scared of them, wouldn't it?' He grins and dashes at the cigarette. 'I couldn't have been too frightened of them if I went out looking for them and then beat them up, could I?'

I can't believe this bloke. Sitting there giving the justification thing a whirl. What gays do with their dicks is their business, I'm thinking, and half because I want to and half to keep things rolling, I give him the homophobia-for-beginners spiel.

He doesn't buy any of it.

'I'm not going to sit here and listen to that crap from you,' he says, leaning forward and staring at me. 'You've got your nice new flat down on Southbank, or South Yarra or somewhere. Am I right?'

I just keep looking at him.

'You've got your girlfriend and she's got her poof chums, who have the facials and love Barbara Streisand and they're friendly with you, too, and they cut fucking hair in Chapel Street and they don't upset your little status quo, do they?'

I sit back. Grab another bit of toast. He's got the hairdresser bit wrong because Thomas, or Tom as I call him, is a chef.

'So what's your point, mate? You don't like gays? There's a bit of that going around . . .'

Max swings into top gear. Tells me about the macho types who hung out in the pubs where he went as a kid—

how they tried to pick him up. Sneaky blokes. Didn't know who they were half the time. No big moustaches like in the movies. Too smart for that. Kept quiet in the corners and didn't stick around too long. Just long enough to make a hit and go. Looking for little fresh ones.

'That'd make for an interesting night at the boozer.'

He doesn't take the bait, just shuts up and goes back to slicing and chopping at his grill. He keeps eating and doesn't say anything, doesn't even look up. I sit and munch on toast for a while and even think about another coffee. I watch him cutting his sausage and wonder how I'm going to get out what I want to say next.

It's one of those times when I wish I *did* smoke. I always want something to hang on to when I ask questions like the one I know is getting ready to come shooting out of my mouth. The boys at HQ didn't tell me everything, but I'm putting two and two together about why old Maxey's up to some new tricks.

'Did one of them rape you?'

Max doesn't flinch but it's like something gets sucked out of the space between us. I work hard to keep my eyes on him. He looks down at his cigarette pack and pulls another one out even though there's still a quarter of one hanging in the ashtray. He lights it and says nothing. Blows the smoke out through his mouth.

I back my gut.

'If you were that young, wouldn't that make the bloke who did it a paedophile, a rock spider—'

'They're all the same, fucken—'

He's raised his voice but doesn't finish, just sits there looking past me. The bloke in the coat looks across at us. Max starts fiddling with his folded up serviette.

This bloke's a case, I'm thinking.

I start imagining Richards in dunnies all over town. He's pounding those chunky fists into little blokes with buck teeth, their lips are splitting and blood's pissing down their chins. Then he's standing over them and kicking them in the balls until their faces are white and they don't know how to scream anymore because it doesn't feel like there's anything left inside their guts to scream with.

I reckon there'd be a time to give old Maxey the stats about gays and rock spiders. But the whites of those knuckles hanging onto his knife and fork tell me now isn't it. Still, I'm worried that what I've got next is going to piss him off even more.

I gallop up to the last hurdle, keeping an eye on his knuckles.

'But . . .' I say and then go quiet.

Max looks at me and puts the fork down and he's only hanging onto the knife. I need this by-line so I've got to jump. I want to shut my eyes.

'Aren't you a bit of a perve, too? You root em now. Rape em, actually . . .'

I say the last bit as quick as I can. Then I do my best to hold Max's eyes.

He stares at me for a long time, rubbing at his eyebrow like the idea that someone might think he's a creep has never crossed his mind. He puts his knife down and dabs at the corner of his mouth with another serviette. Then he goes through his cigarette routine again before he talks. He takes his time and he's almost whispering.

'I said I don't know what's going on.' His eyes flick round the joint and then settle down on Luigi unloading frozen dim sims. He grabs my tape recorder and pauses it. Puts it back down on the table. 'Some of em scream out, "Rape!" and all that sort of crap and whinge about it ...' He keeps his eyes on me. Then he looks down and wipes some leftover egg from his plate with the cold toast. 'But some of em don't ...'

He grabs my recorder and turns it on again. He wipes and wipes at the egg yolk with his toast. When he finally looks up at me again his eyes have gone soft.

I look into those eyes for what seems like a few minutes. I feel like I'm sitting at a swimming pool, one of those ones in the tropics, with all the palm trees around them. I'm pressing my knees together under the table and his lips are sitting flat and red on his face.

Outside, the flow of pedestrians is getting heavier. Max wipes at the plate and doesn't eat his toast. Every now and again he looks up at me and smiles. I don't know what to say and it seems that's good because I don't think he wants me to say anything.

I watch the tape spinning inside the recorder.

Max stops using the toast as a sponge and eats it, looking at me as he does. Then he puts his elbows on the table and rests his chin in both his hands. He looks straight at me and smiles. I'm spooked because as he does I get a buzz in my groin.

'I've got to go,' he whispers. 'Call me if you want to talk again.'

He gets up from the table and I don't know why but I'm watching his legs. I try to take my eyes off this Max Richards. But I'm looking at him putting fifty dollars on the counter and joking with the bloke in the blue coat.

I've got to get into the office, but I keep sitting there looking at his plate, clean and white, not a drop of egg or food or anything on it. The tape recorder hums, turning over and over.

Just before he disappears into the stream of workers, Max Richards catches my eye and smiles again.

I don't smile back.

The Place Where
Water is Made

Skivver left Seasons Hotel and walked to the beach. He sat on the sand for ages, staring at a moon that was tangled up in clouds. Waves broke too loud and behind him palm trees shushed each other. When he wasn't staring at the moon, Skivver stared at clumps of seaweed lying like black dogs on the shore.

He thought about whipping down to Wheeler's Pub to grab a six-pack. But, because it was quarter-past ten, he knew he'd have to buy it across the bar and pay for it through the nose. Then if he drank it he'd have to drive the speedboat back to the island half pissed. So he just sat there and stared out at the island and the neon skull-and-cross-bones sign on the roof of the resort where he worked.

The nightclub out there would be starting to fill up by now. Before he left for Twin Dimms Surf Shop that morning, Skivver saw a ferry-load of girls giggle their way to their rooms. Blonde-haired, stripy pink shirts. Sydney girls.

Skivver took off his thongs and dug his feet into the sand.

At Seasons Hotel, he hadn't even asked Kev what Anthea looked like. Yeah, so she was wearing a suit. But what colour was it? And her hair. Had she dyed it? And what about her eyes? Could looking into them still make you think the world was somehow bigger than sky and sea?

Christ, she'd come out to the island to see him!

Skivver sat and watched the stars and the moon until he felt like grabbing the lot of them, sitting them down and asking them what they knew. About anything. But especially if they knew about what happens when people steal a bit of you. Where do they keep it? If they steal it and don't get caught, does that mean that bit of you belongs to them?

Skivver stood up. He thought about squidging through the soft sand to the pier and the speedboat. He thought about heading back into town.

Then he sat down again.

Eventually everyone works on the island. In year nine, when kids from Tender Reed Bay are riding home with the sun shining on their tanned arms, they look out across the ocean and know one day they'll end up out there on Haymarket, walking among the palms and looking up at the wisps of cloud hanging round the island's peak. The kids know the same hands gripping their racers' handlebars will carry cocktails to fat American women or short-legged and leathery Japanese men, lying on banana lounges smoking thin brown cigars.

But in his teens Skivver missed out on the obligatory pocket-money stint on the island. Instead he worked afternoons at his dad's fishing shop. It earned him enough money for dope and booze, so he left home without even setting foot on the island. He started a degree in primary teaching at Scolby's College outside Brisbane and he was flying until the teaching rounds. Twenty-three stinking grommets with no front teeth yapping at once and he dreamt of a nice cutback on the lip of a right-hander at Tender Reed Bay.

He came back to surf and get his bearings. Figure out what to do next.

Next turned out to be a full-time, live-in job on the island. The resort had a pirate theme and Skivver became a First Mate. That meant he had to make sure the rich and usually unknown had a wild time on the high seas. Between surfing in the morning – and the middle of the day if he could squeeze it in – Skivver fulfilled his job description by banana-lounging with bikinied girls from Melbourne and Sydney who came looking for fun with a tanned and muscular native-type. When they didn't find him, plenty let their bikinis fall onto the white tiles of their hotel rooms for a blond-haired, reasonably toned surfer who was still on the right side of ancient. So many in the last three years that Skivver thought he might knock one back soon.

But the idea of handing out a knock-back became a definite when he heard Anthea Thomas from high school had been out to the island asking for him. And, fuck, wouldn't you know it, it was his day off. Instead of surfing, Skivver was over at Twin Dimms watching Ritchie the head honcho board-shaper work up the new triple thruster he had on order. That board was gunna cook.

Skivver always knew Anthea would come back. She turned up in year nine and left at the end of year eleven. Her father was a developer and he must have finished developing. God knows, Skivver thought, the job was definitely done now. There was hardly a centimetre of beach scrub round the bay that wasn't flattened by a townhouse.

At the end-of-year-eleven party at Katie's place, six of them, including 'Dux of the Year' Anthea, decided they'd sneak off and pinch her dad's boat and motor out to the island's nightclub. Anthea was wearing a thick, yellow singlet that looked white in the moonlight. It showed her nipples dark underneath it, or at least Skivver remembered them being dark and full.

Untying the rope that held her father's boat to the pier, her hair was Cindy Crawford meets just about everything that's sexy, falling down her shoulders like warm honey on toast before you bite it.

Kane Kelly had struck out the week before with Anthea, his first failure in five years of high school. But Skivver didn't give a shit—he was making his move that night, no matter what. He had on his best t-shirt—his white Nirvana one—and his hair was looking so cool that before he left for the party his older sister said, 'How come you don't look like a tool tonight, Skivver?'

The engine stopped a bit under halfway to the island. Kane pulled on both the motors' cords but didn't even raise a splutter. Anthea went to the cabin and checked the gauge they'd all ignored.

'We're outta petrol.'

'Fuck,' Kane said.

Skivver looked at Anthea, who was leaning in the cabin doorway.

'It's your boat. What are we gunna do?'

'We could row back ... Or we could row to the island ...'

It was dark, but Skivver could see her twinkling grin.

Before Skivver found himself sitting on the beach, he'd gone looking for Anthea round Tender Reed Bay. He stopped in at Seasons Hotel, owned by Kev O'Brien, one of his dad's fishing mates.

'Yeah, there was an Anthea here.'

Skivver felt his guts drop, but he kept his face rigid.

'Wend she leave?'

'Sarvo,' Kev said, fiddling with papers on the reception counter.

'You talk to her?'

Kev laughed.

'Yeah. She grilled me mate. I thought she was a fucken journo. Asked heaps of questions bout what was goin on round town you know? Sorta like she was lookin for somethin. But it was like she knew everythin I told her anyway.'

'She ask —'

Kev kept talking as if Skivver wasn't there.

'She wanted to know bout the school. Said she was in the same year as Kane Kelly, the bloke with the Broncos now. I told her where you were —'

Skivver got a word in.

'She came out to the resort, but it was me day off . . .'

Skivver could feel his cheeks sinking fast.

'She an old squeeze of yours, mate?'

Skivver didn't know what to say.

'She's a bit of alright,' Kev added.

Skivver felt a smile start on his lips.

'Bit up herself, though.'

His smiled stopped. 'How's that?'

Kev laughed. 'Well-to-do, mate. Well. To. Do . . .'

Now Skivver managed a smile. 'What was she stayin here for then?'

'Dunno, mate. Roughin it maybe. Seein how the other half live . . .'

'Can't have been that well off,' Skivver said.

'Mate, I've seen chicks in suits but that was some fucken suit . . . Between you and me you gotta worry bout birds in suits.'

An old couple wearing straw hats walked through the automatic doors and Kev stepped across, ready to greet them.

'She say where she lived?'

Kev raised his eyebrow.

'I don't mean open the books, Kev, I mean, did *she* tell ya where she lived? Like when you were chattin?'

Kev smiled.

'Nah she didn't, mate, but I'll take a flyin guess: Sydney. Harbour views pal. She'd drink champers and look straight out at the Opera House.'

Even with long emergency oars you can't row a twenty-foot twin-outboard cruiser. They all laughed and dangled the oars in the water and maybe moved the boat a few centimetres.

'Fuck, you're gunna be in the shit now,' Kane smiled.

Anthea grinned back at him.

'I'll just tell my Dad *you* made me do it . . .'

Kane's smile got swallowed in the dark.

Anthea's thongs clip-clopped as she stepped round the life vests, up the stairs and into the cabin. Light shone across the deck from two huge globes and she stepped back onto the cabin landing. Yep, that was definitely a yellow singlet. And those denim shorts, Jesus!

Anthea laughed. 'It's time to party I reckon.'

After dropping anchor, Anthea disappeared through a trapdoor in the hull and then reappeared, struggling with a small esky. Kane beat Skivver to the task of helping her up the stairs and back on deck.

'The old man keeps a stash,' she said, ripping the paper off the top of a champagne bottle. After the cork flew toward the stars, one of the girls spoke out everyone's fears.

'We're gunna get sprung *so* bad . . .'

'Yeah, I'll be grounded till I leave town,' Anthea said, 'so I'm going to have fun fun fun!'

Skivver was sure Anthea looked at him when she said it.

Her old man had a stash of CDs to go with the beer and champagne. Crap ones: Neil Diamond, The Eagles, and some bloke called Donovan. But they put them on the cabin stereo because it was better than listening to Kane bullshit about how he was going to play for the Broncos. Soon enough he was spewing over the edge of the boat to the tune of the 'Hotel California' lead solo.

Skivver could never remember if he led Anthea into the hull and the bed down there or if she led him. Kane was tongue-pashing Phoebe on the deck after his spew, and Ryan was sitting on top of the cabin, staring at the moon and smoking the rest of the joint he'd passed around.

Skivver's head was full of fog and he stood at the end of the bed, looking at Anthea lying on the doona, with its giant print of an anchor.

'I don't want to do anything. I'm just fuzzed out ya know. Need to lie down,' she said.

Then she sat up and hugged her knees. Skivver could see her red bikini bottoms peaking out of her shorts. He wanted to explode.

'Sit down with me,' she said, smiling.

Skivver sat.

'Do you wanna marry me?'

The fog cleared straight out Skivver's ears.

'What?'

She touched his arm.

'I'm *joking*.'

He looked at the brown cupboard and its gold door handles.

'Look at me, Skivver.'

He looked at her. Then he looked away.

'*No*. Really look at me . . .'

He looked at her again, for longer this time. Then looked away.

'*Skivver*, you're not leaving this bed till you've really looked at me.' She smiled.

He looked at her and he didn't tear his eyes away. He looked and looked into her eyes, long enough to notice that they were channels of blue that stretched into the bay and then out beyond it to whatever makes water in the first place.

She stared at him, too, still smiling.

They stayed like that for minutes or hours. Skivver didn't know or care.

There was a knock on the cabin door, but neither of them could take their eyes off the other or say anything. But if Skivver could have found words he'd have mumbled something about falling down into a pit that was wet and warm at the bottom and then falling through again into something warmer and wetter that he wanted to swim in, drink or just rub all over himself.

The knocking got louder and Kane's voice attached itself to it. He yelled words to the effect that Anthea's father had arrived in a friend's cruiser and was now tin-bottoming his way to the decidedly larger craft he owned.

Skivver never saw Anthea again.

Skivver made it back from Twin Dimms in time for staff dinner.

'There was a chick here today lookin for ya.'

Driscoll gave him the news and a few others smiled and looked in his direction. Skivver stopped eating his plate of lasagne.

'Yeah? Who was it?'

'Some Anthea chick.'

He put his knife and fork down and grabbed his schooner. '*Yeah?* Whad she want?'

'Just asked for ya. I said ya weren't here. She had a look round the joint and bailed.'

'She leave a number or anythin?'

Driscoll grinned. 'Wouldn't you like to know?'

Someone cackled.

Skivver stretched out his arm and started waggling his fingers. 'Hand it over,' he said, managing not to yell.

Driscoll opened the branded button pocket on his pirate shirt. He reached in and then handed him nothing.

There was laughter round the table and Skivver felt his chest go tight.

'Did she say where she was stayin?'

'Nup.'

Skivver left his lasagne and headed straight for his staff apartment.

He put on his best jeans, the ones with the specially made rip above the right knee, and then started flicking wax through his hair.

Where'd she been for six years? Did she live in Brisbane? Did she have a boyfriend?

Nah, she wouldn't have come out to the island if she had a boyfriend.

Was she *really* looking for him? Maybe she was just looking for a job.

He smiled at the mirror. Had her number come up? Was it her turn to work on the island?

Skivver almost ran to the fully lit jetty and the speedboat that nuzzled against it. Driscoll saw him climb into the boat.

'Don't forget you gotta work tomorrow, Romeo!'

Skivver couldn't think of anything smart-arse to say. Once he was away from the pier though, skimming the waves like a stone thrown from a lover's hand, all he could say was her name.

Nesting

She is wandering back and forward in the open space between the biggest of the gum trees. He can see her from his window, high above the park. It's raining, but she's not seeking shelter. Surely someone will come.

Standing in y-fronts and a singlet, Patrick puts his grey suit on a coat hanger. As well as the hint of mothballs, he can still smell dust on the suit, despite all the times he's tried to air it out by hanging it in front of the open window of his fifteenth-floor housing-commission flat.

He slides open the door of a small built-in robe and places the suit on the rack, among pale-blue jeans and a thin, bone-coloured jacket. In the robe mirror he sees a tousle of greying hair, lines on a forehead. This morning, wearing the suit, he looked in the length of that mirror and saw a man who was getting old, but who didn't look too bad for his age. This afternoon he doesn't want to look long enough in the mirror to see, even for a second, what the assessors saw, what they must have seen every time he sat in front of them.

Patrick takes a pale-orange shirt from its hanger. He's

about to shut the door when he decides it's probably stupid to hang the suit unprotected in the robe. It was dusty and smelly when he first started using it again after the years it had been hanging there. What if he wants to use it again?

He puts his shirt on and looks at the suit, hanging side-on in the robe. He lets out a sound that's halfway between a sniff and a grunt. There's really no point hanging the suit up at all. He's not going to use it again.

He's sure that somewhere he's got one of those vinyl zip-up suit covers. He'll find it eventually, put the suit inside. Then he'll fold it away, maybe in the bottom drawer of the dresser. Come to think of it, the suit cover might be in that bottom drawer. He pulls it open and rummages through yellowing newspapers, old socks, manila folders with photocopies spilling from their sides, and black-and-white photographs. One of the photos flicks out from under a manila folder and Patrick's ex-wife smiles at him.

He notices her grey lips – which he remembers were bright red that day in the gardens – and that black beehive hair-do, not as black in the faded photograph as it was when he peered down the lens of his bulky Kodak and said, 'Smile, honey, it's okay', and she did, for once. He holds onto the photo, looks at it for a few more seconds, then places it back under a manila folder.

Patrick takes two steps and he's in the kitchen, grabbing his pack of Holidays from the faded orange bench top and pulling a chair across his small square of dark-green carpet.

He sits down and opens the window. A quick blast of cold air enters the bedsitter and on the coffee table the newspaper and donation forms from various charities rustle for a few seconds then settle.

He lights his cigarette and inhales. What a view. Even if his investments had survived the crash of the early nineties he couldn't have afforded a view like this! On a clear day he can see the wispy outlines of Geelong on the horizon, or at least the smoke from the factories encircling the provincial city. On those afternoons Port Philip Bay is blue-green and yachts scatter across the sea.

But on the horizon this afternoon, storm clouds are building that will eventually knock back the heads of the palm trees on St Kilda Esplanade. The clouds will billow grey until finally, hours later, they'll blacken and invade Patrick's entire view.

He puffs smoke through the open window. Despite having seen the old photograph, he's not sure why his brain has bothered to dredge up the memories: his wife's affair, the divorce, his anger at never receiving children from her ... and then on and on it goes: his inability to love another woman since, the vow of celibacy he took eleven years ago, the lonely nights ...

'Blah, blah, blah,' he says out loud, and grinds his cigarette butt into an aluminium ashtray on the windowsill. He stands up and pulls the chair back to the centre of the carpet, between the front door of his flat and the window's sky world, greying at the horizon, but with some blue and white above the bay and the trawlers cutting through grey-green ocean.

He pulls his coat over his head and walks up to her. The girl is sitting on the wet grass now, crying. She speaks but Patrick can't understand the words. Either they are not English or she hasn't yet learnt to speak meaningfully. He doesn't know how old she is. She seems the age to still hold teddy bears or large dolls, but she has nothing in her hands. Patrick smiles and offers his hand and she looks at it. He whispers and finally she takes it. He leads her to the glass doors at the bottom of the high-rise flats and into the lift.

In between the clouds there are seagulls white-capping the blue, flying higher and higher, spiralling in flashes of sunlight. Patrick watches them rise then fall. He sees their movements every day and knows them as movements within himself; the careening up through clouds, the diving down toward the earth then spiralling upward again: the gulls are independent, yet part of a flock, drawn down to the ground by food scraps and then back into the air by the sheer love of sky, cloud, sunlight.

He's not sure if seagulls have nests or if they just hug themselves close to rocks on the beach. Either way, he imagines they keep mainly to themselves. Yet gulls spend time together; they are not alone. They climb in pairs through the blue, wings almost touching, then tumbling free of each other's vigorous flapping, then wing tips in range again, about to press together, like the fingers of God and Adam in Michelangelo's painting.

Sitting in his chair in the afternoons, Patrick speaks to the seagulls, and sometimes he speaks beyond them into the sky, with words and sometimes without any sounds at all.

Patrick has never seen young seagulls. Are they kept hidden away until they're capable of fighting for hot chips thrown from picnic gatherings? Perhaps on beaches throughout the world, high up on rocky cliff faces, there are caves where adult gulls care for their young, keeping them fed, preparing them for the rigours of food competition and the glories of flight.

She drinks milk from a glass and he stands with her at the window. Patrick points at the seagulls, still flying in the rain. She's stopped crying and she mumbles and points with him at the sky.

He thinks of his suit in the cupboard, whether he might search again for the plastic cover. He shifts in his chair and looks at the blackening horizon and as he does, for the first time in the eleven years he's lived in his flat, he takes special notice of the sparrows sitting on the window ledge. Three, then two, then four. Little observers at the window. Wings fluttering.

They've always been in his view, but out of focus, like a piece of dream you bring into the day. They've been there, peeking in, while the soaring gulls drew away his attention. Patrick walks to the window, the sparrows scatter and he looks up and down the ledge. It's covered in droppings – white, grey and even darker in places. He goes back to his chair and one by one the birds return.

He stares at them for a while and then drifts off and before long he's feeling his penis through his y-fronts, slowly rubbing. The act stopped being sexual years ago. He works away for a little longer on the outside of his underwear, thinks about letting his hand dive under, but doesn't bother. There'll be nothing on TV later, he'll need something to do.

Today he looked the best he had in years. His grey suit was well matched with a white shirt and a tie that was a slightly darker shade of grey than his suit. He'd seen that look in a magazine he'd flicked through in the doctor's waiting room a few weeks ago. Nothing else had worked, why not try fashion?

One of the assessors, Leanne, he'd met several times so he said hello. A woman with flowing blonde hair, she smiled back. The second one, an older woman with brown hair in a bun, he'd never seen before. He smiled at her and she nodded, but her face remained blank.

'Thanks again for your application, Mr Thomas.'

'No problem, Leanne.'

'We've really considered it very carefully.'

The other woman looked down at her papers.

'But we're going to have to reject it again, I'm afraid.'

Three months he'd spent on this application, got advice from Terrance Martin, his old friend from teachers' college, now turned big-time lawyer in Collins Street. It wasn't easy to get Terrance on the phone, but when Patrick told him how many times he'd been rejected, Terrance said it sounded like discrimination, and he offered to help. But what bloody good had it been?

Patrick shook his head. 'Why?'

He addressed his question to Leanne, but the other woman looked up. 'Mr Thompson –'

'*Thomas* –'

' – we have to consider every aspect of the child's development. And, really, there remain several reasons why we can't allow a child in your care at this time ...'

Patrick had heard all the reasons before, but he raised his voice. 'What? What are they?'

On the way home on the tram, Patrick sat stiff-limbed and above the heads of passengers he looked through the tram's windows, imagined his fist smashing through every one of them, the glass shattering and spilling out onto the tracks to be crushed by the tram's steel wheels. People would move to stop him and he'd send them sprawling to the floor or across the seats.

He sat with his eyes lowered and his lips slightly apart.

His fists stayed clenched by his sides, a collection of foul language on the end of his tongue.

We have known Mr Thomas for eleven years. We believe we can offer an independent assessment of his character because there have been thousands of us in this period of time who have witnessed details of his life. If required we can also provide notes taken at our meetings held in trees throughout Melbourne.

Mr Thomas is, we suspect, a surrogate member of our kind. He sits for long periods nested high above the city, he disappears and then returns to that position. We have also noticed the many hours he is perched and contemplating the movement of our seagull cousins. We hear him speaking and we are becoming more and more convinced of both his sage qualities and his natural ability to blend with the sky. His speaking is both aural and inaudible and its subject matter is not only himself and his willingness to transform into something, it seems, even *more* like us than we are, but also about the city he is perched above and the many landing grounds to which our kind and thousands of others migrate every year. We believe his coming and going and the kindly, settled nature of his dark eyes, are convincing evidence that he is not far removed from our family.

He is rather large, but we have not noticed him use his weight and size in an untoward manner. We have noticed the often-frantic attention he gives his reproductive organ, but we have never noticed anyone present when he attends to this natural process; a process we see as especially necessary, considering the fact that we have never seen Mr Thomas with a fully mature member of the opposite sex in his nest, though other semi-mature members of the same sex have been known to visit with him, carrying basketballs.

I hasten to add that we cannot provide any further assessments because Mr Thomas seems increasingly aware of our presence. We will continue, however, to visit his nest. We all gain immeasurably from the warm paternity and wisdom that flows from him. Wingless he is, yes, but given to flight.

Patrick sits in his chair, watches the seagulls tumble. Outside, the afternoon is beginning to hold its breath. The leaves on the palm trees lining the promenade give an occasional dispirited wave, and even the sea has relaxed a little, no white caps bobbing for attention.

He could flick on the portable TV later, watch it spill its guts in multi-coloured images. Or he could, more likely, sit in silence, watching and listening as the storm parades its flashes of light and drum rolls across the bay; watch like a wide-eyed medieval peasant at a guillotine execution as the storm builds and empowers itself, talks up the punishment it's going to mete out to the ocean and any boats foolish enough to still be on the bay, the punishment it will visit on the palm trees, then the shops and apartments and finally, the housing-commission flats and the people inside them, the one man watching the day disappearing, wanting the neck of this day to be sliced under the weight of a blade so powerful it can cut through stone and rock and then extend itself through suburbs to cosy, two-storey homes and find those who deny others the chance to love, cut them down, slice them up, rain on them forever.

But today, neither TV nor storm watching seem good enough uses of Patrick's time.

With his mouth closed he strokes his front teeth with his tongue, then breathes out. Were they sparrows just then, on the ledge? He walks to the window. Nothing. An empty ledge above apartments and houses turned to face the sea, the coming storm.

Patrick takes his cigarette pack from the windowsill and puts it in his shirt pocket. He pulls some pants on and goes to the fridge: jellies – green, red, yellow – all in white bowls, untouched, above a packet of white bread.

He goes outside and sits on the park bench for a while, won't go over to the kids playing basketball today. Two of them wave and he waves back. The ball flies through the air to the smallest of the kids, wearing a red singlet over a black windcheater, and the kid shoots two points. The whole gang waves at Patrick and he smiles and salutes them.

He's seen plenty of men sit on park benches, just like this, and though he told himself he never would, now that he's resting here it's not as he thought it would be. It's almost natural. He understands them now, the men in overcoats, their packets of bread, their fingers diving into them, the congregations at their feet. He opens his packet, takes out a slice and breaks it into little pieces. He throws them at his feet and waits.

Perhaps it's because of the approaching storm, but no birds arrive to peck at the crumbs. The basketballers head for the open glass doors at the bottom of the high-rise flats and step inside. On the footpaths, people in suits and neat skirts scramble along the footpath, umbrellas in hands but unopened. The orange streetlights flicker on and soon it's dark enough for their oozy orange glow to fill the park.

Patrick's wondering where the storm has got to, what's causing the hold up, when he looks down at the sparrows, their orderly approach to the bread, pecking, stepping back, pecking. He smiles at their manners, congratulations them out loud.

Soon seagulls careen in from their hiding places and he notices with a smile that some gulls appear to be smaller than others. The sparrows step-hop back, then try to hold their ground in the chittering and squawking.

The bread packet in his lap, Patrick smiles and withholds its contents, twisting the plastic bag that holds the slices. With gentle words and a soothing voice, he waves his finger and begins to sort out this family squabble. And he's sure that for just a few seconds the birds are silent.

The girl is sitting on Patrick's chair, watching TV, eating green jelly from a white bowl. Patrick sees the group of people below, searching behind trees, walking across the grass. There are two policeman in the group and several more in long coats running in. He'll take her down soon, when he's ready. He'll take her.

Finding My
Mother's Magic

Cups of tea blew steam into the air and Aunty Flo scratched her chin. She looked at Mum across the kitchen table. Mum sat with her elbows resting on the table and her hands covering her nose and mouth. Because she didn't sit like that very often, I remember it more than shivering in the dark and cold when we started to walk home.

Mum was usually too busy around the farm for any sitting down at all, let alone resting in what I think of now as her had-enough pose. I caught her at it other times when she didn't know anyone was watching. She'd sit there for a few minutes, moving her hands up and down her nose and sighing into her fingers. But that night was the first time I'd seen her doing it with anyone else around.

I scuffed my shoes on the dirt floor and looked at them both. Mum didn't seem to notice that the rain was getting heavier. She didn't call my brothers in from the porch. She'd said they could play out there, just for a few minutes, if they put their jackets and hats on. I don't think she wanted them inside. She never let them play outside, ever, on nights that cold.

My eldest brother, Peter, had disappeared into the barn. I wondered whether he might go and comfort Fella, my horse. He was really Peter's, but when I was five, I liked to think Fella was mine. I knew he'd be scared with the wind starting to pick up. The paddocks were all thick up with cloud and dark and Fella was probably running away from the wind hooting at him out of wire fences. That was if the sound of gum trees wrestling with each other wasn't enough to scare him.

'So Harry's out there in the car on Grampians Road and he just let you lot walk home?'

Aunty Flo stared across the table.

'Yes,' Mum said, stretching the word out and rubbing her head. 'When we broke down he said he was stopping there for the night. And he just lay back and before I knew it he was snoring. I couldn't get out and try and get the car going myself. And I wasn't going to stay out there all night with the kids. They'd have bloody froze.'

My mother looked at me. She didn't swear much. Not in front of me. She didn't want me turning out like one of those loose-mouthed larrikins that hung around Brian Woodford's shop. Whenever she swore in front of me she said, 'Sorry love, don't listen to that.' Tonight she just looked at me and gave me the smallest smile I'd ever seen and said, 'Go and play in your room will you please?'

'That's a good lad,' said Aunty Flo, taking a big slurp out of her cup and putting it down.

I liked Aunty Flo. She was big with flabby arms and when she gave you a hug you felt like you were snuggled up in clouds. She looked after us sometimes when Mum had to help our father in the paddocks. Aunty Flo wore a straw hat, always, with flowers strapped into it. Her dresses, too, were always covered in flowers, mainly red ones. That night she was driving home when she saw us all walking in the dark. She picked us up and brought us back to the farm.

'Go on Neville, get going.' Mum's voice was louder.

I ran off into the lounge but didn't go straight to the bedroom I shared with two of my elder brothers. There was something about the way Mum and Aunty Flo were talking that made me want to be around them.

The kitchen was quieter. Normally the two of them would let knives and spoons clatter in the sink and they'd talk to each other like they were sitting at opposite ends of the town hall. That night they were quiet with their cups. They landed them like sparrows on the saucer after every sip.

I looked through the kitchen door at them from where they couldn't see me. Aunty Flo was looking at Mum and Mum was looking down at her tea like she was worried about something in her cup.

'Nancy . . .'

Mum didn't look up.

Aunty Flo had a look on her face as if she was carrying something really heavy and couldn't find anywhere to put it down.

'You know you should think about leaving him.'

That made Mum look up. She moved her head forward as if she might answer straight away and then she was quiet for a long time.

Finally she said, 'Oh, don't be so stupid, Flo. What would I do?' She stopped then and rubbed her finger into her eye. 'And where would I go? I haven't got tuppence to rub together.'

We'd driven down to Natimuk that night where our father drank on Fridays. It was a little town with a lake in the middle of it and two pubs. But only one of them was any good. So our father said.

Normally he drank at home, but Friday nights he got together with his war mates, some still in their uniforms, and the drinking was special. You could hear it through the white frosty windows that reminded me of Christmas. At least the Christmas where Santa was.

On Friday nights our father would sometimes come home happy, talking about the opportunities all over the place. 'You just have to look,' he would say. 'By jingoes, you just have to keep a look out.'

It was different to hear him talk like that.

Because Mum wasn't allowed in the pub it was Peter's job to go in and tell our father we were there to take him home. After a while, Mum let me tag along with Peter.

The first time I went in there, I stopped in the doorway, too scared to go any further. The whole room was full of orange light that seemed brighter than any light I'd seen before. And men were everywhere like I hadn't seen them before. Laughing and talking, sometimes slapping each other on the back.

After the first time I got my courage up. I pushed through the door as it swung shut behind Peter, and the yelling and laughing sprang up and wrapped its arm around my shoulder, whispered jokes and told me I was a big sonny Jim. Then it pushed me along until I got to Peter and the bar stool where our father always sat.

My father rubbed me on the head when I walked up to him. Every time he would introduce me to Bluey Thompson who sat next to him, with big round arms and blue pictures on them. Back then, I thought that was why they called him Bluey.

Before we left for the car my father gave me a sip of his beer. He never did it at home. 'Seeya later, Harry,' half the men in the pub called out as we left. And because our father picked wild flowers on our property for a living, some men yelled out, 'Watch out those flowers don't turn you into a dung puncher!' I didn't know what that meant then, but my father responded by saying, 'No worries about that fellas' and pushing his hips back and forward.

I left the pub that Friday the same as every other, but with the taste of beer in my mouth and my father almost crushing me underneath his hand, sounding happy and like he might stay that way.

I had plenty of memories of how he was on Friday nights stacked up in my head like books. I pulled one out whenever I went to bed with my head stinging from knuckles or my bum cut and bleeding from the belt. Or when I was trying to get rid of the memory of Mum lying on the ground where she'd fallen, our father over the top of her saying what it was like to have to put up with her and all of us kids.

I knew that having good memories in your head was better than talking about what happened at home. Because what happened at home, stayed at home. That's what Mum said. 'Don't you be telling anyone about what goes on in this house, Neville. What goes on here doesn't concern anybody else, anyone nosing around in our business.'

We have to forgive our father. That's what we have to do, we have to understand. We don't realise what it was like in the war. We don't know what it was like to have guns going off all day. Or to have someone put a bayonet in our stomach and one more twist of the blade and that would be the end of us. We have to forgive and be on our knees at night and pray for our father.

Maybe that was what my mother did when she put her hands up over her face and sighed into them. She was praying with just her breath.

Mum and Aunty Flo whispered then talked louder then whispered. Mum rested her head on her hands. Aunty Flo took her hat off and held it on her lap and looked down at it.

If I'd snuck a bit closer to the kitchen door, I could have heard more of what they were saying. But I'd had enough of listening. I knew what my mother needed so I got myself busy.

I turned up the cushions on the couch, hunted underneath it and found bottle tops, but they weren't what I was after. I searched under the radiogram and in behind the cabinet that held all our best crockery, the one I had to be careful of whenever I ran past it. I stretched my hand along the wall as far as I could reach and dragged one out.

'You bewdy,' I said to myself.

Only one so far, though. I needed another.

I tried in the hallway, in behind the teak chest where Mum kept all her sewing things. I pulled out a steel mousetrap that had gone off long ago and missed the mouse. I reached my hand in further and touched something that seemed promising. I strained my arm as far as it would go and managed to pull it out.

A copper button. Great for coats, but no good for me.

There had to be another one somewhere.

There would be one in the kitchen for sure. I knew Mum and Aunty Flo didn't want me in there, but this was way too important. I had to risk it.

I snuck in, hoping they would be too busy talking to notice me. Mum was looking down again. Aunty Flo saw me, but it didn't seem to worry her that I was back. I crawled along the wall and reached in behind the meat safe and stretched until I thought my arm would break off. But it was worth it. I'd found another one.

Forgetting what might happen to me, I ran over to where Mum was sitting, reached up and put the coins in front of her on the table, right next to her teacup.

'Look Mum, tuppence! Now you can leave.'

Mum looked at me as if I had an extra ear or something growing out of the top of my head. Then she raised her eyebrows and looked at Aunty Flo. She put her hat back on and straightened her dress.

'He must have heard what you said about not having a penny to your name,' Aunty Flo whispered, pressing her lips together.

Instead of yelling at me to go to my room, Mum let out a little laugh.

'Thanks, love.'

I waited for her to rub them together. What magic they had in them I didn't know. But they had to be special if she could do it and leave the farm. She'd take me and my brothers. Peter had better get in from the barn.

'Rub them together, Mum.'

She sat for a few seconds and didn't say anything. Aunty Flo stood up and gave me a little smile.

'Come on, Neville,' Mum said and she got off her chair and pushed it under the table. 'Let's round up those brothers of yours. It's time for bed.'

'Think about what I'm telling you,' Aunty Flo said.

'Yes,' Mum said, with something like a smile on her face. 'It'll be alright to pack the bags now, won't it, with my tuppence and everything?'

I knew it. Those coins were magic. And I had found them. But she walked away and left them on the table. I followed her onto the porch.

'Mum, your money . . .'

It was like I hadn't spoken at all. She just told my brothers to get up and go inside and told me to shut up now about my tuppence.

TJF

Female by hangin's a rare one. I'd heard of it, but never seen it. Birds usually do the deed with tablets.

I waltzed up to the tree in Footscray Park that night and me partner, young Constable Sheldon, was there already. Still puffin cos he'd sprinted to get on the scene. The bloke who'd called us was there, too, with his big Alaskan-lookin dog. One a those things you don't wanna go near less ya havta.

'Approximately what time did you first see the body? Have you seen this woman before this evening?'

Shelly drilled the bloke with the usual crap and the bloke said stuff back with his voice all shaky.

'Yes, I saw – no I haven't seen – I got the call – I mean I called you . . .' and he bullshitted on.

'Bruises all over her, Ron,' Shelly said. 'And her clothes are ripped at the back.'

Fuck, I thought. Now we can't just pencil down she's topped herself. Possible evidence of a struggle. Gotta call fucken homicide and we could be here all night.

Shelly asked the bloke if he'd touched the body and thank Christ he hadn't. We were gunna be there long enough without another shitload of paperwork. The dog barked at a possum piss-fartin round in another tree and then the bloke piped up again.

'Is there anything else I can do, guys? Call someone or something?'

As if me and Shelly were stuck in the desert with no way to get onto anyone.

'No thank you, sir,' I said. 'Thanks very much for your assistance. However, Constable Sheldon has all your details and we'll be in touch if need be.'

The usual bullshit.

'Thanks for getting here so quick,' the bloke said, as if he'd had a whole heap of shit to do before we got there.

He whistled the dog and it pricked its ears, ignored him, and then on the second whistle it got its act into gear, off behind him, puffin a heap of mist into the air and pissin on everythin.

I've been back at work about a month now. Just drivin a desk around, fucken non-operational. But, Jesus Christ, it's better than bein at home. Too much time to think. Too much catches up on ya. After they stuck me on sick leave, I was fucked all the time and I could hardly get outta me chair.

Just like in here at compliance, but at least there's people around and I'm startin to talk to em a bit. Plus if I keep me mind busy nothin much else can get in there. Keep things loud enough in me brain and nothin can get in there yappin.

So I try and keep busy sortin out bloody letters from people whingin about their speedin fines: 'It wasn't me in the car that day, someone else was drivin it.' I just tell em to send in the names and addresses of everyone they live with and if that doesn't scare em off I let em go. Couldn't give a fuck.

But the skinny prick who runs the show here could.

'Ron, could I meet with you about eleven o clock? I've just gotta iron out a few process things ... Is that alright, mate, is that okay?'

I'll iron *him* out.

'No worries, Al.'

He only gives me half a smile cos he likes everyone to call him *Allistair*, but he can shove it up his arse.

I'll probably forget to meet him anyway. I can't remember where I've left the paper or me car keys or anythin these days. When I'm not forgettin stuff I'm gettin all churned up about all sorts of bullshit. What time's lunch? Am I gunna miss it? People will talk to me and I won't fucken hear em. And when they stuck me on leave I was sittin at home in the lounge in the middle of the day lookin at the telly but not turnin the fucken thing on. And then after a while, shit, I turned the thing on alright. Bloody loud. Or the stereo ... Anythin to keep her quiet ... Fuck.

Shrink reckons the whole thing's got somethin to do with everythin I've seen on the job in thirty or whatever years. He reckons that's what buggered me up that night with Shelly and the bird hangin in the tree. But if that was right there should be hundreds of cunts like me. All non-operational. But they're fucken not. They're out in the trucks or down at forensic or even ridin the bloody horses up Bourke Street.

'Ron, have you got your footy tips in yet? *Ron*, have you got your *tips* in yet? Do you want me to drop em in for ya?'

'Here they are mate, sorry, hang on . . . I didn't tip your shithouse mob . . . I hate the fucken Dogs. EJ was a bloody thug far as I's concerned . . .'

I tell all this to Leon and grin at him. He's not a bad bloke. He's been out in the trucks, not like half the other blokes in here. I mean, every second day out there some crap goes on that could make you go stupid in the head. But, shit, that's the job. I mean, fucken hell, that's it. What else? Stringin dandelions together?

You get on with it. You don't fuck around. If it all gets a bit much you go down the boozer and tell a few war stories. Some of the young connies take fat black textas with em and write TJF in the dunnies.

The Job's Fucked.

I said to Shelly that night, 'Call the station for the camera, will ya', and he just stood there lookin at the body.

'Come on mate, get cracken. And get some tape while you're there if we've got some.'

Shelly took off and then I looked at the body and thought it won't matter if there's no tape. With the bloke and his arctic fucken wolf gone, hopefully no other bastard will turn up and wanna play totem tennis with the body or anythin.

I laughed out loud and it sounded a bit strange cos the park was empty. Like me laugh should have gone somewhere but it got nabbed in the dark.

Constable Stupid came back after a while, puffin.

'Camera's not at the station, Ron.'

'Where the fuck do they reckon it is? Didn't they run a gear check this mornin?'

Shelly didn't answer any of that. Stood there like a stale bottle of piss. And he didn't want to look at me, the bastard.

'Where's the camera, pal?'

He didn't answer again for a bit. Then he must have thought, Fuck it, I'm gone, I may as well not drag it out.

'I leant it to my sister.'

'You're fucken jokin.'

Shelly didn't say anythin. Just looked down.

'What the fuck for?'

'She needed a digital one for uni. Just for the day ...'

'For fuck's sake ... And she didn't bring it back?'

'Nup.'

I informed the young constable, the same young constable who I was pretty sure about a month before had a bit to do with a little investigation into yours truly over an incident at the Rising Sun Hotel, that I could have his fucken arse on report.

'I know,' he said.

I stared at him for a few seconds. Then let him off the hook.

'But I won't.'

He looked down and I could hear him kickin around in some leaves. I didn't talk to him for a while until I figured out what to do.

'There's an all-night chemist somewhere near bloody Barkly Street or maybe somewhere up that way. Anyway, go and buy one of those throwaway camera things.'

He started to head off.

'And don't pay for it ... and grab a pizza, too, while you're at it. Aussie and whatever shit you want.'

He stopped and looked at the body.

'She's not goin anywhere, mate.'

I gave him a grin but he'd already made tracks.

I hung around waitin for him and I remember offerin her a smoke. Said, 'Want one, love?' and laughed. Maybe that's what pissed her off. I don't know.

I remember sittin down against the tree for what seemed like ages, and I got this real heavy feelin in me chest. It wasn't heart trouble, I know that. I was just lettin out really deep breaths and at the same time feelin like more than air was gettin out of me. After a while I felt fucken alright again.

I was flick flick flickin away on me lighter cos the wind had sprung up when Shelly turned up out of the dark and I hid the lighter away quick. I smelt him comin first, big waft of egg and cheese.

'You're frightened. You're a scared, weak bastard.'

'What the fuck did you say to me?'

Shelly handed me the camera and one of the pizza boxes.

'I didn't say anything.'

'You weak, scared bastard.'

'Listen, smart arse. I'll fucken give you one, don't doubt it.'

'What for?'

'You know what for.'

The next time I heard him say somethin to me I was lookin straight at him and his lips weren't movin. I turned around behind me and the dead bird's eyes were open and I saw that it was her lips goin at it.

And that's all I remember of the night. That's it.

Constable Shitforbrains shouldn't have come in here yesterday. Why did he think it would end up in anythin but trouble?

He dobbed me in for what happened that night. And I've been put off for six months and holed up with a shrink every week. Then he comes all the way over here to Compliance tryin to smooth things over. Fuck off.

It was always gunna be a blue once we started goin over it all again. The six fucken bullets missin from me gun and the six fucken bullets in an already dead body.

He says he's sorry they whacked me on sick leave. But he couldn't do anythin else but report me. Went on and on about it.

I got sick of it and told him to shut up. And I shoved him.

I didn't *punch* him. It just made everythin look bad when a chair went over and he cut himself on the side of a desk.

'Ron, I want to meet with you now, if that's okay ...'

Al's got a look on his face like he's been tryin to get through to me for a while. Judgin by how quiet every other bastard in the office is he probly has.

'Come with me please, Ron. We've got a meeting, mate.'

I'm up nice and quick and headin toward the glass panels of his office.

'Ah, mate, nah ... We're meeting down ... Down in one of the other ...'

He leads me down the corridor to the white door on the end, to the left. He opens it and sittin there is Ian Jackson from Special Investigations and Brian McFadyen, with his bald head and glasses, all the way from fucken HQ. I stand at the door and say to meself they can't take me commendations away, they can't do that.

I walk in and I can already see meself sittin in me lounge room in the middle of the day with the telly off. And then I'll be turnin it on as loud as I can cos she'll be back once I'm outta here, you can betcha balls, she'll be back at me, yappin, and next thing I'll be seein her blue jeans and skimpy top at the window.

So I stand there in front of McFadyen and Jackson and I could be cryin, I'm not sure. And if I am it's cos I'm thinkin, I'm gunna need me gun at home with me this time you bastards.

Acknowledgements

Stories in this book have been previously published, some in different versions, in the following journals and anthologies. Thanks to all the editors.

'A Grandfather's Reminder' – *Overland*, No. 177, Summer 2004.

'In the Shell' – *Island*, No. 97, Winter 2004; *Best Australian Stories 2004* (Black Inc.).

'Cappuccino, Soft Drink and the End of the World' – *Deathbed Challenge*, Sleepers Publishing Almanac, 2005.

'Driven from Darackmore to Toonenbuck' – Overland, No. 173, Summer 2003.

'Talisman' – *A Family Affair*, Sleepers Publishing Almanac, 2007.

'The Favourite' – *Island*, No. 102, Spring 2005; *Best Australian Stories 2005* (Black Inc.).

'The Hero' – *Beyond Words*, The Ada Cambridge Prize for Biographical Short Story Writing Anthology, 2006.

'A Redundancy' (under the title A Redeployment) – *Overland*, No. 165, Summer 2001.

'Nesting' – *Antipodes*, Vol. 20, No. 1, June 2006.

'Finding My Mother's Magic' – forthcoming, *Quadrant*, 2007.

'TJF' – *Normal Service Will Resume*, Cardigan Press, 2003.

'The Favourite' won the 2004 University of Canberra National Short Story Competition. 'The Hero' was highly commended in the 2006 Ada Cambridge Prize for Biographical Short Story Writing. 'Driven from Darackmore to Toonenbuck' and 'A Grandfather's Reminder' have been broadcast on the ABC.

Author's Note

To the following people, thanks for your support in so many different ways over the last few years: my family, Kylie Ashenbrenner, Mike and Kathy Bond, Jo Bowers, Mark Brett, Clare Boyd-Macrae, Jo Case, Nick Carah, Alistair Cashmore, Christy Dena, Martin Flanagan, Ilsa Hampton, Mark Holt, Andrew Kinnersley, Simone Mitchell, Al Macrae, Ryan Paine, Paul Wiegard, all the crew at Wakefield Press and all the workshop participants and tutors at RMIT way back when I started dreaming up these stories.

Wakefield Press is an independent publishing and
distribution company based in Adelaide, South Australia.
We love good stories and publish beautiful books.
To see our full range of titles, please visit our website at
www.wakefieldpress.com.au.